SEND JUDAH FIRST

The Erased Life of an Enslaved Soul

By Brian C. Johnson

Hidden Shelf Publishing House
P.O. Box 4168, McCall, ID 83638
www.hiddenshelfpublishinghouse.com

SEND JUDAH FIRST

Cover art: Megan Whitfield

Graphic design: Ali Kaukola

Interior layout: Kerstin Stokes

Library of Congress Cataloguing-in-Publication Data

Johnson, Brian C.
Send Judah First

ISBN: 978-1-7338193-1-2

Printed in the United States of America

"Compelling, haunting, horrific and beautiful. In *Send Judah First*, Brian C. Johnson has crafted a novel that brings vividly to life enslaved people – Judah, Aunt Sally, Truelove, Anthony... – that so many have tried to erase from American history. A heart-wrenching and essential story."
> - Thomas Norman DeWolf, author of *Inheriting the Trade,* and co-author of *Gather at the Table* and *The Little Book of Racial Healing*

"*Send Judah First* is a wonderful piece of historical fiction. Drawing on a small number of surviving historical records, Brian C. Johnson paints a beautiful portrait of a woman in slavery in nineteenth-century Virginia and provides great insight into their life and work. Joh son boldly exposes some of the very worst aspects of human bondage – sexual abuse, physical punishment, and the mental anguish of reconciling the Christianity of the southern masters with their own treatment as slaves."
> - Jennifer Oast, associate professor of history, Bloomsburg University, author of *Institutional Slavery: Slaveholding Churches, Schools, Colleges, and Businesses in Virginia, 1680-1860*

"As Belle Grove researches the lives of the men, women, and children who were enslaved here, the story of Judah seized our hearts. We are so pleased that it has inspired the heart, imagination, and talents of Brian C. Johnson too. Although we still have many questions about the lives of Judah and her children that we hope to answer, this story brings her to life in a magical and powerful way. We can't wait for you to meet her."
> - *Kristen Laise, Executive Director at Belle Grove Plantation*

TABLE OF CONTENTS

DEDICATION

To the countless number of enslaved men and women whose names have been erased, blotted out, and forgotten because of America's "peculiar institution." Your stories, their stories, our stories must be told, not glossed over, hidden, or forgotten. I may have never met Judah, but she is me and I her.

FOREWORD

I first "met" Judah on Saturday, October 16, 2016. As part of my responsibilities as director of the Frederick Douglass Institute for Academic Excellence at Bloomsburg University of Pennsylvania, I had led an overnight student field trip for a living history weekend at Belle Grove plantation in Middletown, Virginia.

After disembarking from the bus, our guides led us to the plantation's winter kitchen, a lower level room with a big fireplace. A woman dressed in period attire stirred pots hanging in the fireplace, preparing our dinner. Kristen Laise, executive director of the plantation, introduced Ranger Shannon Moeck of the National Park Service, who would tell us more about the woman who had occupied this space for nearly four decades in the early 1800s.

The program was titled "Kneading in Silence: A Glimpse into the Life of Judah the Enslaved Cook." Shannon provided an overview of the laws governing life of the enslaved in Virginia and spoke of Judah's children.

We were told about the multi-layered work of the enslaved cook, who not only prepared the food for the master and his family, but also for all the enslaved workers. I felt a kinship to Judah. I love to cook.

Shannon also showed us some of the cure-alls and soaps the cook may have made in her role as medicine woman and slave doctor. Holding those items was a spiritual experience. I know Judah likely never touched them, but I felt her willing me to connect with her.

And then came a detail that nearly broke my heart—there are only two existing documents that prove Judah ever lived.

Send Judah First is based upon my knowledge of slave history and what is in the Hite family historical record. The

6

legacy of slavery is alive in America today. As a nation, we celebrate/mourn/acknowledge, in 2019, the 400th anniversary of the first arrival of Africans as slaves to Virginia. America, as a nation, must grapple with this "hard history." Clarion calls and nods to the U.S. Constitution fail to acknowledge that the Founding Fathers, including the first five presidents, were slave owners. President James Madison, chief author of the document declaring America's commitment to equality called slavery "the most oppressive dominion ever exercised by man over man." By the way, President Madison saw blacks as three-fifths a person. Madison makes an appearance in this tale, as he was the real-life brother of Nelly Madison Hite, first mistress of Belle Grove.

There have been times when I have felt inadequate to tell Judah's story. At other times, I feel like no one else should or could tell her story. I feel called to it. Shannon encouraged us to "imagine life for Judah and her family at Belle Grove . . . years of working, living, raising a family under enslaved conditions."

Send Judah First is not a tale of scandal, of insurrections and violence, but of one woman's attempts to live with dignity above the negative circumstances of forced servitude. This story gives honor to a woman (and all those like her), who suffered the indignities of oppression and racism, but did the ultimate—she survived. Not as a weakling, but as resilient and determined.

SEND JUDAH FIRST

-1-

"Yuda! Amkeni!"

Awakened by her mother's fearsome screams, young Yuda stood frozen as she struggled to find her sense of direction.

"Mama, Ni nini mbaya?"

Mama yelled for Yuda to run, but which direction? She tried to fight the sleep from her eyes and the nighttime clouds out of her brain. Mama's fearful voice turned to anger as Yuda seemed to move too slow. The acrid smell of burning filled Yuda's nostrils . . . fire! Yuda could hear the villagers running wildly in fear. Strangers had invaded the village.

"Kuna wageni katika kijiji," her mother screamed.

"Wageni? Ni akina nani?" Yuda questioned, trying to corral her confusion as a ball of fire came flying into their home.

"Yuda, sasa! Wao ni kuchoma kila kitu! Sisi lazima kukimbia sasa!"

"Mama, nyumba ni kuchoma!"

"Yuda, kukimbia!" At her mother's command, Yuda rushed outside, barely seeing the stock of a stranger's rifle, the impact slamming the bridge of her nose, her thoughts shattered.

When she came to her senses, Yuda was being marched alongside a train of other black bodies. Each had been tied to the other like a string of baby elephants. Horrified and crying, Yuda desperately scanned the crowd.

"Mama! Mama! Nini kinaendelea? Anakozi? Kwa nini ni sisi kuwa minyororo pamoja?"

What was happening and why were they chained?

And who were these African men barking orders in a language she did not understand. What village were they from and why were they yelling? One of the men walked close to her.

"Yeye anasema nini?"

Perhaps he would explain. Instead, he pulled out a small crooked stick and pointed it in the air, producing an awful crack of noise as smoke poured from the front of it. The man looked at her with an anger she had never seen, as if he were not even human.

Hasira ya pepo!

Yuda saw her friend, Anakozi, walking near to her. Anakozi had screamed when the weapon went off, trying to put her hands over her ears. But movement was impossible with their hands chained. The strange men kept pushing, hitting, yelling. But then she saw something she had never seen—a man of goat's milk, his face and arms oddly white. The man waved one of his hands as if ordering everyone to move while speaking in Yuda's direction.

"Sasa! Hebu kupata hatua ya juu!"

What? Yuda was stunned to hear this abnormal looking man using her language. Perhaps this was one of those goat's milk men of another religion she had heard about. The elders had warned not to trust these strange men who had been taught by demons to destroy life.

"Hofu mgenim," the elders had said. "Mgeni atatuangamiza na kuharibu nchi yetu."

Yuda had thought the elders of unsound mind, but now realized they were right.

Abioye suddenly held up the line, pointing to his mouth.

"Mimi nimechoka na kiu hivyo!"

An African jabbed him with a pole, but then commotion broke out at the front of the line. Dinka, the warrior, was attempting to pull himself free from the chains. But the boom of a fire stick scared him back. Yuda had never seen Dinka afraid of anything.

Through the trees, Yuda heard waves crashing against the beach. She knew they were getting close to the Great Sea. When they reached the clearing, she saw three large ships docked near the shore. Lines of black bodies shiny with sweat in the sunlight were climbing aboard the ships, still locked together in chains and ropes. Men and women alike screamed out the names of their children, but the waves drowned out their voices.

And now she noticed many men with faces of goat's milk, all with fire sticks. Having never seen white men before, except for the one on the trail, Yuda's gaze locked for fear.

Yuda saw Lakshmana, her cousin, at the top of the ship on the right. She thought to call out to her, but by the time she found the words, Lakshmana was gone.

"Yuda!"

Turning toward the sound of her name, Yuda caught a

glimpse of her mother's face in the sun, standing among a crowd of prisoners.

"Mama!" Yuda screamed with the fierceness of a warrior and pulled at her chains. Yuda expected her mother to do the same, that such a strong woman would have put up a mighty fuss as they shackled her. But, when Yuda got a better look, she only saw the agony of a tired and beaten woman with downcast eyes, dragging her chains. Mama looked up again, her eyes wanting to pull her daughter closer, her voice carrying dimly across the distance.

"Yuda, jipeni moyo! Sisi kupata njia hii. Mimi ni daima na wewe!"

Yuda wondered how her mother could smile and tell her to be of good cheer. In her twelve years of living, Yuda had never been separated from her mother.

"Mama!" Yuda called out, but she was gone.

Yuda's eyes burned from crying as she was led aboard the third ship, past white men with anger in their eyes and words. As one man barked loud sounds with no meaning, she noticed brown drool dripping from his mouth. Yuda tried to turn away from the sight, her mind racing with ideas of how she might escape. No, it was impossible.

Her chest ached and the chains made it difficult to walk up the long plank onto the ship. A hard shove forced her to keep moving forward. Onto the deck of the ship, some of the women were released from their chains and pushed into a room. Everyone else was sent down into a dark hold.

In the scant light, Yuda seemed to be surrounded within a dense crowd, a human cargo of maybe two hundred others in her same condition. In the obscurity, she noticed each man and boy being blatantly shoved and locked onto a line of shackles that were fastened tightly to the inner walls of the ship. The women and girls were cordoned off away from the men and pushed into a large and dusky room, the only light coming from cracks in the wood. They were not chained, but the door was closed and bolted.

A few minutes later, the large door overhead slammed shut, leaving nothing but darkness, fear, and agony. There was so little room to move and her entire body throbbed in pain.

Between the cries and groans of her fellow captives, Yuda thought she heard the scurrying of feet on the upper level. And then, the ship lurched forward. Yuda felt dizzy and sick as her body adjusted to the ship's movement in the waves. She clutched the wooden wall with one hand and her stomach with the other. It had been hours since her last meal, but she still had to fight to keep her stomach contents down, even while others could not.

Who were all these people crammed in the darkness? Yuda did not hear anyone who spoke her language, who might be from Goga.

"Ni mtu yeyote kutoka goga?" she cried.

"Yuda?"

The voice was barely audible and came from the other side of the wall. Somehow, it broke through the commotion.

"Yuda, ni kwamba wewe?"

Even though it came with the sound of chains being pounded against the wall, the voice was beautifully familiar.

"Dinka?"

Yuda's heart felt stronger. He was not that far away,

just the other side of her wall. She could not see him, so many bodies in the dark, but felt safe knowing Dinka was nearby. The cloaking shroud of fear and uncertainty abated; Dinka would protect her.

The ship sailed for quite some time before the big door pulled open and a flood of sunlight poured in.

"Hiyo inaumiza!"

Yuda and many of the others cried out in pain as their eyes adjusted to the invading light.

Two men of goat's milk descended the stairs and opened the door to the women's cell. Smiling, they leered and pointed at the women and young girls. One white man with a mouthful of crooked teeth grabbed his manhood and pointed at Yuda. She tried to turn her body to hide but could hardly move it was so crowded. She was but a girl, her body still developing, too young for such stares. But Crooked Teeth kept looking at her.

Je, meno ya mviringo yanataka nini?

-2-

M any days must have passed. Yuda had never seen or felt such horror. The stench of being locked within a damp chamber; crammed against bodies unknown. Sorrow, anger, fear, frustration—she cried for days, deeply longing for her mother, her father, her brothers and sisters, her friends. Would she see any of them ever again? And what was left of her home, of beautiful Goga? Even spurts of sleep, twisted atop the damp floor, brought no comfort.

Death was everywhere. At times, groups of captives were dragged onto the deck and ordered to dance around to the delight and abuse of the white men. A few of the Africans managed to break free, jumping into the Great Sea to drown. Some refused to eat and were force fed. Others simply wasted away into death, their bodies producing a rancid smell that lingered long after the goat's milk men had removed the corpse and tossed it into the ocean.

Both Yuda's body and mind felt shattered.

Ambapo walikuwa wao kwenda? Kuibiwa kwa kuchinjwa? Mimi watakufa?

Where were they going? Stolen for slaughter? Would she die? It was the fear of the unknown that shook her core.

Eventually, the ship began to slow, the trap door opened, and the blinding sunlight once again poured in as the white men came down the steps, yelling in their strange tongue.

"Look alive, you black bastards! Time to get up. Rise and shine. Time to get y'all ready for market. We gonna have us a lot of fun!"

Her eyes had barely adjusted to the brightness as she was prodded up to the deck.

Yuda felt the grime under her elongated fingernails. Bits of crust had dried between her thighs. Gogans were proud people and the filthiness of her covering cloth brought her great shame. She pulled at her matted hair as her skin crawled from the smelly memory of the woman next to her who had soiled herself when she was unable to get to the bucket the white men had given them to collect their waste.

On the deck, Yuda inhaled the fresh crisp air, the first clean air she'd smelled for so long. Her moment of refreshment was spoiled as a bucket of cold water was splashed into her face. She sputtered the water from her mouth and looked around at her companions. Water droplets glistened on their deep, dark brown skin in the sunlight as the white men gleefully tossed bucket upon bucket of water upon them. Her brothers and sisters began washing off the stench from weeks in the jela—a jail. Having seen elephants bathing like this, she assumed that's what the white men expected them to do.

Still, the feeling of water felt liberating, as if Yuda was a normal person once again. But that feeling would be momentary. After another splash, she gasped and took in a couple deep breaths. Shaking the water from her face, she looked ashore, wondering where she was and what possibly could be next.

While they were bathed, Yuda felt the stares of Crooked Teeth, a disgusting white man stealing the joy of the warm sun on her skin. Again, she wanted to cover up and hide. Although she had tried to rid her mind of his disgust, she again felt unclean, contaminated. She had tried to protest and fight, but Crooked Teeth had dragged her out of the women's jela and into a corner out of the men's view. It was good not be be seen, she thought, as he violated and shamed her at his pleasure.

Uchafu kuudhi. Yeye ni mnyama.

Her *matiti* had begun to swell and become very sensitive. In fact, they hurt. She recalled asking her mama when her bumps would grow. Her mother had told her that when she became a woman, the little mosquito bites on her chest would become rounder and fill up like hers. Yuda thought she must be a woman now.

Yuda once again was overcome with the sick and empty feeling of yearning for her mother.

After being washed, the captives were given clean clothes to wear. Although the cloth was scant, Yuda felt grateful to be covered up. When her face had dried, she glanced across the horizon. Several large ships had docked. She could tell this was some bustling seaport or marketplace, yet no women were around with baskets of sundries balanced on their heads. This was not Goga.

Again, the white demons chained everyone together and herded the long line down the ship's plank and into a large wooden room with a dirt floor. It wasn't long before several white men entered and unleashed the binds upon their wrists, ordering everyone to strip off their clothes. The white men then slathered the naked bodies with some greasy substance. Yuda took notice of the fire sticks hanging at their sides.

"Gonna shine you niggers up for market. Fetch a pretty penny."

Once greased, the shined people were permitted to put their clothes back on. Yuda noticed a white man she assumed must have been a king based on his royal dress. His fine white mane tumbled down his back from underneath a triangular hat with a feathered plume. He talked quietly with another man. They looked at something that appeared to be sheets of extremely thin wood, but Yuda had no idea why the two men found these sheets so fascinating. They shook hands and the king walked away with a large smile on his face.

Just then drums started to play. White people who had been milling about began to gather around a stage set in the middle of an outdoor courtyard.

The same man who had shaken hands with the king began to speak.

"Wonderful people of the south, can I beg your attention? Welcome to Norfolk. As advertised, on this beautiful autumn day in the year of our Lord, 1807, we have a superb lot of choice cargo, healthy slaves largely from the Volta River near the Ivory Coast. They've made a safe passage and are in prime, healthy condition.

"One other note of significance, with this new and, I think we can all agree, brazen federal law going into effect on the first of January, this may be one of your final opportunities to buy full-bred African stock. But the good news is that your purchases today will quickly grow in value. So, let's get this very strong batch of niggers up here."

A white man unlocked the holding cage and the line of blacks, still tied together, was dragged to the center of the square. One by one, each was released from the line and escorted to the stage.

"We'll start with the wenches," the leader bellowed. "Let's whet your appetites with a few prized wenches. If you desire to inspect any of the items being offered for any defects, blemishes, or sickness, you can do so at your pleasure."

A younger black woman was pulled from the group first and white men poured over her. They first grabbed her face, pulled her jaw open, and inspected her teeth.

"This young negro wench is a fine, black pearl indeed, and she's in superior condition. You'll find no marks; she's young and supple. She'll give you a great return on your investment. No doubt, you'll get years of service out of this one. She can wash and clean, sew, be set out to be a field picker, plow, what have you."

Within seconds, the men started ripping at her clothes until she stood there stunned and naked. Laughing and smiling, they bent her over and began exploring with their fingers.

Yuda watched in horror and humiliation. Her fear of shame quadrupled as the realization hit her that her turn would be coming soon. Would they do the same to her?

Kuacha! Kuacha! Hii ni sawasawa na zaidi ya aibu.

But the leader would not stop. Instead, he began talking with a quick tongue, sounding like the men who sell vegetables and fruits in the market back home. Soon, he slammed a large hammer on wood and they dragged the young girl away.

The display of women and girls continued. Even her friend, Ngozo, was shamed and taken by a white man from the crowd.

Yuda was next.

Loosened from the ropes, she was pushed to the stage.

Hii haiwezi kuwa. Usiniguse. Mimi ni mtoto.

"Oh, gentlemen, a fine nigra lass we have here. She'll make a superior fancy maid. She has the childbearing hips that will keep you warm on a chilly night. Inspect away, gentlemen."

Yuda had no idea what he said, but her tunic was immediately drawn away and pulled over her head, her body once again exposed to the world. She felt like *mnyama*—an animal—as a man cupped her *matiti* and several others rubbed their hands against her body, but Yuda felt relieved to not be finger-explored the same way as Ngozo and many of the other women.

As they backed away, Yuda wanted to scream with fear and sadness. Yet, for some unknown reason, she smiled.

"Well, this one apparently likes to be handled," the leader crowed as laughter spread through the crowd. "Who will start the bidding?"

As he had done previously, the leader now spoke very fast, pointing toward different people in the crowd as they raised their hands. His words still rambled until *bang*, "Sold. A fine purchase by the gentleman from Tidewater."

A man moved forward and tugged at her arm but allowed her to put her tunic back on before dragging her to his wagon. Yuda felt thankful to be out of the center of the square, but she didn't want to go with this man.

"Komesha hakuna!" she cried, dragging her feet. "Hamjambo nyote!"

No one came to her rescue.

-3-

T he man tossed Yuda into the back of his wagon like a sack of fruit, not caring that her left leg hit the cart. She wiped the trickle of blood with the bottom of her tunic as the driver shouted for the horses to move. There were nine others in the wagon with her. Yuda pleaded with them to tell her where they were going.

"Tunaenda wapi? Tunaenda wapi? Ambao ni watu hawa?"

They didn't answer.

Je, mtu yeyote kujua lugha yangu?

She recalled the loneliness of the ship, longing for real communication with someone, anyone. She kept trying.

Perhaps the man driving the cart would answer her questions. She pulled at the corner of his shirt. "Tunaenda wapi?" No response. She tugged again. "Tunaenda wapi?" He turned sideways and smacked her hard across the face.

He angrily spoke, his words making no sense. However, she understood his intent: sit down, stay quiet, stay alive.

"Mtu muovu," she said quietly.

Her wagon-mates sat with the stillness of hippos basking in the mud. She noticed two *wapiganaji* who were certainly capable of fighting this man; warriors who could easily come to her aid and be her protector, even though they were chained. Still, no one had helped when Crooked Teeth spoiled her all those times. Now these men simply sat there while this cruel man had slapped her face. The elders of Goga would be ashamed of these men.

Watu hawa hawana heshima.

Yuda glanced at the driver, her face still throbbing. She envisioned breaking her chains, grabbing the large white man and throwing him off the wagon.

Mimi wangepigana wewe mwenyewe kama ungeku-wa si mara mbili Saizi yangu.

Yuda settled down in the corner, purposely attempting to ease her mind. She watched the trees as the wagon made its way down the dirt path. Birds flew by and she longed to feel their liberty. Nothing was holding them down.

She pulled the iron chain wrapped around her ankle cutting into her skin. She tried to pry the metal apart, but it would not budge. She yanked harder, but the iron ring held its grip tight. One of the others pulled her hand away, a silent warning not to pull at her chains.

Over time, Yuda fell asleep. She awoke as the horses began to slow. Looking off to the right, she noticed they were approaching another wagon stopped on the road.

The driver stalled his horses alongside and the white men talked to each other. A few minutes later, an unfamiliar white man grabbed Yuda's ankles and chains, pulling her from the wagon. Once he had her standing, he indignantly shoved her into the back of his wagon. He did the same with three other captives, linking their chains with more chains.

"Thanks, Norman," said the new white man.

"Sure James, but I need to tell you that I am not doing this anymore."

"This hopefully will be the last time. I think that slaves direct from Africa are so much stronger and a better purchase than those bred in captivity. Since I moved to Alexandria, things have been tough. On my life, I swear to pay you back every shilling with interest when it all turns around."

"It doesn't make much sense to add onto your property load if you're having such adversity." Norman's face bespoke genuine concern.

"Things are a bit different for you down in the Tidewater region," said James, "but I need more folks to plant more fields. It's the only way I can grow and prosper. It'll all work in the end. Thank you, old friend. I am in your debt."

James Shields shook Norman's hand, loaded up the wagon with his new human goods, and started off on the three-day journey to his farm.

Food and water were minimal along the way, the captives each chained to a tree at night. Finally, James spread his arms and said, "Welcome to Alexandria. Your new home."

A swarm of black folks appeared to welcome the travelers. An elderly man pulled at the horses until they slowed to a halt. He seemed happy the white man had returned.

"Welcome back, Mastah James. You sho' have been gone a mighty long time. We's mighty glad to see ya. Who us got here?"

"This here is Absalom," said Shields, slapping the back of the large muscular man. "He's going to help on the farm."

Chained to Absalom was a boy not much older than Yuda.

"And this youngin' is David. We'll put him out to work in the fields."

He pointed to the girl latched to Yuda.

"And this is Faith. I've been told she can sew. We'll put her to work with Marnie."

That left Yuda.

"This little pretty is, how'd they say it? Ya . . . do . . . or something like that. We'll just call her Sukey. She's gonna help with old Aunt Sally in the kitchen. Malachi, you be sure and get them acclimated to their new surroundings. Get them up to speed quick-like or I'll tan your hide."

"Yes, Mastah, I'll learn 'em real good."

The white man handed Malachi a key and watched as the links were released from the four newcomers. The shackles, however, remained around their ankles, so each was still dragging a chain.

He returned the key and Yuda watched the white man walk toward a great house.

"Y'all get on now," Malachi said to the foursome, none of whom understood his language. "Let me show you round."

Malachi led the way across the large expanse of land, walking the team past large plots of vegetable plants. Yuda figured that one large field of leafy green plants must be important, what with so many men and women harvesting in baskets and sacks. She also noticed a muscular white man watching everyone work.

"Mastah Thomas, this here is David. Mastah James said

he's going to work out here with y'all." Malachi turned to David. "Boy, you get on ova here and greet Mastah Thomas. He you new boss. You mind him good now."

The tour continued. As they approached a barn, Yuda saw several men—black and white—trying to hold a horse steady, attempting to keep its mouth open.

"Old Lightning ain't been eatin', so we needs to feed 'im so he doesn't die on us," said Malachi to the confused newcomers.

The man grabbed what looked like a snake with a cup on the end and the new people gasped. "Hold him tight, boys. When we put this down his throat, he's gonna buck something awful. Hold him still now."

Yuda figured the snake must have bit the horse's tongue because he jumped and made an awful sound. The black men wrestled the horse, trying to keep him still. The white man put some sort of mash into the cup on the end of the snake and tried coaxing it down into the horse's mouth.

"C'mon, Lightning, you have to eat now."

The sight of these men fighting with the horse reminded Yuda of the ship. On one occasion, three white men had grabbed Dinka. He had continually refused to eat the yellow mush and now the white men had forced open his mouth. Crooked Teeth pulled out a wooden plug and inserted a snake in the middle. They poured mush into the snake while Dinka choked, spit, and bucked just like Lightning.

Malachi's foreign words broke Yuda from her horrified trance.

"C'mon gal. Let's keep it movin."

Malachi escorted Yuda inside the great house. With fire

sticks in about every room, she wondered if he was expecting a war.

Ni yeye kutarajia vita?

Malachi indicated for Yuda to stand still and then yelled through the doorway.

"Aunt Sally, Mastah want you to meet somebody."

Out walked a dark-skinned old woman, wiping her hands on her apron.

"Who Mastah want me to meet now? I'm trying to get suppah ready and y'all botherin me." Her bottom lip poked out and she spit a bit of brown juice onto the ground.

"This here is Sukey."

Aunt Sally looked at Yuda with disdain.

"I done tole Mastah James I doan need no hep! Now, he done brought this gal heah. She gon get in my way. I bet she doan even no nuttin bout cookin. How she gon hep me?"

"Settle yoself down, Aunt Sally. Doan be so rude. You knows you can't see too good no moh. You already done burned yoself in the fire. Mastah say you need de help."

"Hmmph!" She again spit some brown juice.

Malachi laughed. He did not seem fazed by Aunt Sally's ire. She didn't seem to care too much for Malachi either. She looked Yuda up and down.

"What you say her name was agin?"

"Sukey," said Malachi.

"Sukey, huh? Can you cook Miss Sukey?

"Unaweza kunisaidia?" Yuda wondered if Aunt Sally would help her get home.

"Lawd today! She doan even talk Anglish! She still talkin like she in Africa."

"I guess we gon have to teach her." Malachi smiled at Yuda with a fondness she had not felt since Goga, since her father—her wonderful baba. Looking at Malachi, she yearned for home. Last she remembered everything was on fire.

She shivered, feeling cold and alone.

"Samahani, mimi miss mama yangu," Yuda pleaded. "Je, unajua yeye yuko wapi?"

"Lawd," Sally interjected, "I doan know what us gon do wit this gal talkin like dat."

-4-

S uddenly, a group of white men with several ropes were dragging a slim black man roughly through the field. His body was covered in sweat and he was breathing heavily.

"Hang him up against that pole there, boys. We gonna teach this nigger about runnin away."

The white men wrapped his hands around a metal hook and secured the ropes tightly. Master James stormed from the house, carrying a whip in his right hand. On the ship, Yuda had thought it was a long black snake that the white men cracked.

"Jasper, where was you going, boy?" asked Master Shields. "You trying to run away from us, from your family? You know that's against the rules. Now I gotta make an example outta you. Malachi?"

Malachi came running.

"Yes, Mastah?"

"Get everybody together. Jasper wants to show y'all something."

"Yessuh."

Malachi ran off calling various names and returned with a lot of black folks running behind him, inquisitive looks on their faces.

Master Shields paced and announced to the onlookers, "Jasper here wanted to take a trip into town. And for some strange reason, he thought he was gonna get away from us."

Shields turned to Jasper, tied helplessly to the pole and trying not to shake.

"Did you think you was gonna leave your home? This is where you belong." His grip tightenedon the whip. "Now, maybe this will help you remember your place. Get that shirt off him."

The white men ripped the shirt from Jasper's back, the sweat on his shoulder blades glistening in the late afternoon sun.

"Please, Marster Shields. I's so sorry! I's nevah do it again."

"I know you won't." James pulled back and swung the whip in Jasper's direction, as if that snake bit into the poor boy's back, red blood bursting out and dripping down. Master Shields swung a few more times, the skin on Jasper's back ripped like shreds.

"Heat up that brand, boys."

At the command, one white man—Master Thomas from the field—smiled a slick, greasy smile and went over to the campfire, stirring up the coals in a flourish of grey smoke and orange flames. Soon, Master Thomas brought a glowing piece of metal over to Master Shields. A woman began to cry, the crowd wheezing in anxiety and fear. Yuda bowed her head and gritted her teeth. She didn't know what would happen next but assumed the worst.

"And just in case any of you forget where you belong,"

Master Shields continued, "and *who* you belong to, let this be a reminder."

Master Thomas plunged the glowing stick into Jasper's flesh, the young man howling in pain. The onlookers gasped, Yuda just as shaken. Malachi quickly turned toward her with a stern face as if to say she should mind her emotions. She quickly contained herself, not wanting to anger the one person who really seemed to care about her.

When the ordeal was over, Malachi pulled Yuda off to the side.

"Miss Sukey," he whispered sternly. "When Mastah Shields is teachin a lesson, you mind yoself." He tightened the grip on her arm, emphasizing his point.

All afternoon, Yuda fought back tears trying to force Jasper's painful yelp out of her head. He had been beaten so bad he could barely stand, but to have a symbol burned into his back seemed unnecessarily evil. In the cabin Yuda had been assigned to, a woman named Minerva applied a black salve to Jasper's wounds while another woman, Suzy, tried to get Jasper to drink water from a tin cup. Each time Minerva applied the ointment, Jasper lightly jumped and sucked air between his teeth. Yuda made it up in her mind that she would never do whatever Jasper had done.

Yuda watched the healing ritual with interest. She didn't want to be in the way but wanted to offer help. She sat close by, afraid to move, her heart hurt so much. Seeing people branded was nothing new to Yuda. It was part of her tribal ritual, but not like this. Back home, to be scarred was a mark of honor. But this was repulsive, immoral.

When Minerva completed her nursing, Yuda laid her

head near Jasper's to let him know she was there, that she hurt with him. When she saw a rag hanging from the side of a bucket, she dipped the rag in water, wrung it out and laid the cloth on Jasper's forehead. She had done this several times before Malachi interrupted.

"Sukey, given all this fuss with Jaspah, best we lock you up fo de night. It be for y'own good. We doan want you wanderin off."

Malachi grabbed her arm and led her to a chain hanging from the cabin wall. Esther, an older woman who slept in the corner of the cabin, brought some water.

"It be okay, chile. Dey jes want you safe."

Yuda did not understand the words but was calmed by the warmth in Esther's voice. As the light dimmed at sunset, Yuda began to think of the slave ship and Crooked Teeth. She fought her fright but wondered how the morning would be different. If only these days and months were just a dream and she would wake up back home.

With the crowing of the rooster, Yuda opened her eyes to the bloody back of Jasper. It had not been a dream.

Esther shook Yuda's shoulder.

"C'mon, chile, time to get de day started. Deres much to be done befoh the white folk get up. Les get you some vittles. Gotta keep yo strength up."

Esther beckoned to Malachi, who was standing on the front stoop.

"Come loosen dese chains up, Malachi. Sukey gotta do her bidness."

After he had released her from the wall, Yuda's arms fell to her side like weighted irons. She massaged her shoulders and stretched her limbs. Esther motioned for

Yuda to follow her. They walked to the rear of the cabin to the site of a large hole dug in the ground. Esther straddled the hole while lifting her skirt. The pungent stink of morning urine caught the faint breeze while it dripped in a heavy stream and pooled in the hole. Yuda turned her face against the direction of the wind. When Esther was done, she motioned for Yuda to do the same.

"You now, Miss Sukey."

Yuda looked around shyly, wondering if others would be able to see her, yet she followed Esther's lead. The presence of strangers took a backseat to the tightness of the morning bladder.

When they had finished, Esther brought Yuda to the front porch of the cabin where several others had gathered. She opened a cloth bundle to reveal what seemed to be a bounty of food.

"Y'all come on and get sumpin ta eat. Aunt Sally done fixed us up a hearty breakfast."

The group gathered around Esther and began to gobble down each morsel. Sukey slowly bit into a biskuti; it was fluffy and delicious. She could see why the others ate so quickly. Whoever made these was truly gifted. There was also some mushy stuff that reminded her of the food on the ship. She refused it.

"It's a good day, y'all," said a burly man. "Mastah done gave us meat for breakfuss."

As he reached for the food, Auntie Esther slapped his hand.

"You forget your manners, Franklin? Miss Sukey first."

Esther motioned for her to take a piece of meat. Yuda loved the taste.

"Ajabu," she squealed.

Auntie Esther reacted to the smile on Yuda's face.

"You like that bacon, Miss Sukey?" Yuda continued to scarf down the delicacy. "Well, doan get used to it. Dis doan happen dat offen."

Off in the distance, a loud bell rang several times. As Yuda turned her head in the direction of the sound, the breakfast friends quickly cleaned up their spaces, washed their hands in the nearby pail of water and rushed off in various directions. Auntie Esther stayed back to clean the dishes and straighten up the cabin. Her care of the others reminded Yuda of the village *bibi* who helped raise the children and teach the young mothers the way of the world.

Malachi returned.

"Miss Sukey, I've come to collect you and get you ready for the day. I hope you've eaten well. You gon be busy today."

As they walked past the garden, Malachi grabbed a tool and began to hack at the ground.

"You know anything about gahdenin, Miss Sukey? When you get up each morning, this will be your job to ten to de vegetables."

He grabbed a basket and began to pull vegetables from the vine, acting out each instruction.

"You take the ripe vegetables and collect dem here in this basket." He hacked a few more times and then laid the tool up against the fence. "Then, you carry this basket into the kitchen for Aunt Sally so she can cook dem up for Mastah and his kinfolk."

The garden was close to the kitchen area.

JOHNSON

"Mornin, Aunt Sally," said Malachi. "I've got Miss Sukey here for you. And we got today's harvest. Whatchu cookin?"

"Nevah you mind what I's cookin. It ain't fo you! Now ain't you got somewhere else to be, Malachi? Leave this chile be. If'n I have ta work with her, I reckon we better get stahted."

"Why, yes ma'am! I'll get right out of your way. Miss Sukey, doan you worry, she ain't gonna bite you."

Malachi leaned close to Sukey as if he was telling her some great secret.

"She a sweet old lady. Jes set in her ways is awl."

-5-

A unt Sally stared at Sukey as she stood in the old woman's kitchen. The grey cloud in Sally's right eye bore the evidence she could not see very well, but still left Sukey feeling like an invader.

Sukey figured she might ease the tension if she thanked Aunt Sally for the delicious breakfast.

"Asante kwa ajili ya kifungua kinywa ladha."

"Honey, if we gon work togethah, you is gonna have to learn how to speak. I doan understan dat African talk."

Sukey was slowly picking up this foreign language, but it was confusing. She tried to ease the communication barrier with body language. Sukey would pantomime eating something, rub her stomach and smile. Sally enjoyed the attempt and smiled a toothless grin, mumbling some words that were not nearly as stern or mean sounding as before.

"Oh, honey, doan menshun it. It's my lot."

Small talk escaped them. Sukey studied the older woman, trying to figure out Aunt Sally's age. She seemed worn and old yet moved about the kitchen with confidence and ease.

"Lawdy, I done lost the day," Sally suddenly gasped. "I

gotta get lunch stahted. C'mon heah, gal." She motioned Sukey forward. "First thing you gotta know bout de slave cook is we belongs to dis fire! Doan you nevah evah let dis heah fire burn out." Sally pointed again and again to the fire burning inside the hearth. "All day, every day, we is here, tendin the fire. Summertime, it's hot, but you doan let this fire go out." She wagged her finger at Sukey and shook her head. "Winter time, you'll thank the good Lawd for dis fire. You cook night and day. We cook for de white folks an we cook for the nigras. You get up fo de sun to cook an you cooks all day. At night, you dream about what you be cookin de nex day."

Watching Aunt Sally move about the kitchen, it was clear she took great pride in her work, as if her life centered around preparing wonderful meals. No wonder she didn't want Sukey working in her domain. Even though she sensed Aunt Sally might be beginning to like her, Sukey knew she had yet to prove herself.

When she lived in Goga, Yuda had helped her mama prepare the food every day. In her village, young girls helped to make the milo. Mama always let her make porridge for breakfast. In fact, Yuda would cook large pots of it so they would have enough for later meals to be served with meat or fish and vegetables.

At home, Yuda knew she could cook. But, here, she was Sukey. And the nervousness of being in a new place with Aunt Sally breathing down her neck and inspecting every little thing she did served up a lot of pressure. Perhaps part of Sukey's problem was that she wanted to please Sally so badly. To Sukey, Aunt Sally was queen of the kitchen, deserving great respect.

Aunt Sally alikuwa malkia wa jikoni, wanaostahiki heshima kubwa.

Someday, Sukey hoped to be a malkia wa jikoni.

* * * *

Aunt Sally stirred something in a pot. Sukey quickly ran over and mimed that she wanted to help. At first, Sally shooed her away, but Sukey would not be discouraged. She grabbed at Sally's spoon and pulled her arm. She finally wrenched the utensil away from Sally's tight grasp and started stirring the big pot. Sukey stirred like a master; at least that's what she thought it looked like. She was wrong.

"Gal, you bettah get out of my face and get outta my kitchen. You doan know nuttin bout cooking for white folk. You gon get us both whipped."

Aunt Sally made a shooing motion and grabbed Sukey's shoulders. "No, get out! Get out!"

"Hakuna! I si kwenda!"

Sukey refused to leave. She would not abandon her assignment. She could not fail the *malkia*. She had already witnessed what happened when the *bwana* was displeased. And he had assigned her to help Aunt Sally.

"Tafadhali kuweka mimi. I wanaweza kujifunza. Nipe nafasi nyingine!"

Sukey cried and pleaded with Sally to give her another chance. She would learn her way of doing things.

"Tafadhali, Malkia." Sukey protested pulling at Sally's skirt tail. "Tafadhali!"

Auny Sally turned away and started pulling out jars and

pouches from a nearby cupboard. She pulled a pinch of something out of a little brown pouch and sprinkled it in a pot and started stirring. She didn't say what it was and Sukey didn't ask. Of course, she didn't know how to anyway. Sukey chuckled as she thought about that.

"Mebbe there's some use for you afta all, Miss Sukey. Okay, I's gonna teach you how to make Mastah's favorite hoecakes. Say it with me, hoe cakes."

Sally righted herself, stood Sukey up straight and grabbed her cheeks with both hands. She pointed at her own mouth. Sukey reasoned Sally wanted her to follow her lead. Sally made a circle with her own lips and Sukey could feel little breathy puffs of air. She tried to repeat Sally's words exactly. "H-h-h-h."

"Right, now add this sound, ooooo. Put dem together, Hoooo-cakes."

"Hoe c-c-c-akes."

"Dat's it. Yous gettin it."

Sukey smiled when Sally smiled; laughed when she laughed. She worked hard to earn more praise, even if she still didn't understand what Aunt Sally was saying. After all, her parents had taught her that wisdom is like fire that you take from others.

Hekima ni kama moto. Watu kuchukua kutoka kwa wengine.

Sukey watched Sally make the hoecakes. First, she mixed flour with a white powder she called "sugah" and a yellow-ish grainy powder she called "coanmeal." She also poured in maziwa. Sally went to the fireplace and poked at the white coals. After fitting three square stones together, she laid a black skillet on top.

"Get dat skillet hot and we can fry us up some hoecakes" Sally beamed. Sukey was entranced.

"Now wit dis spachla, we gonna peak at de otha side of the hoecake. An when it look good, we jes flip it for a minute or two so we's cook both sides. Master love dese things. He eat dem up whenevah I cook em."

Aunt Sally continued the lesson. She pulled Sukey like a toy doll all over the kitchen to grab various items.

"Gon teach you ta talk Anglish," she said.

Sukey watched as Sally took the lid off a jar and stuck her hand down into a white powder that she scooped into a *bakuli*. Next, she grabbed Sukey's left hand and dipped it into the cold powder. Sukey mimicked Sally and dumped it into the *bakuli*.

"Flour," Sally said, pointing to the powder in the bowl.

The powder was a little different than Sukey had back home where they ground their own with a stone. They made *unga* after the ngano had turned brown at the tops. The children went through the field to collect the buds and brought them back to the women who smashed the buds into a fine dust. That dust had been used to make the *mkate* they ate with each meal.

Next, Sally took *chumvi* from a small jar off the table and sprinkled some of the white sand into the *unga*. Reaching into a jar, she brought out some of the greasy stuff the white men had smeared on Yuda's skin at the marketplace. Sukey took a step back, her mind once again envisioning the horror.

Aunt Sally laughed, "Ain't nothin to fear, chile. This stuff is the cook's best friend. It bring nothin but good."

She pulled Sukey to the dark area in the corner of the

kitchen. Plunging her hand down in the water, Sally pulled out a *chupa* and poured *maziwa* from the cow into a *bakuli.*

"Milk," Sally dictated, pointing to the liquid.

"Malk," Sukey mispronounced, causing Sally to chuckle.

"Milk, chile. You gets it someday."

Once the *maziwa* went in the mixture, Aunt Sally reached her hand in the mix and stirred, not even trying to reach for the spoon. The *unga* clumped up and got stuck to Sally's hand. Sukey tried to stay out of her way, but that didn't work. Sally grabbed Sukey's hands with her sticky white fingers and dipped Sukey's hands into the muck and bid her to stir. At first, Sukey didn't like the mixture, but the more she stirred, the stickier and drier it became. Instead of mush, it looked like small beads.

When the concoction seemed appropriately mixed, Sally wiped their hands off with a rag and poured a different liquid into a pan she had setting on the fire. Into that, she dumped the contents of the *bakuli.* The liquid made a bubbling sound. Sukey tried to listen closely, but Aunt Sally pulled her back.

"Sukey, honey chile, you can't get so close to that hot oil. You'll get burned fo sho."

Sukey paused, remembering her mother's warnings about being safe near the open fire.

Aunt Sally put the pan further back onto the coals, but not directly on the fire. Sukey noticed Sally kept a pot of *maji ya moto* on the fire that she used to periodically clean her area as they cooked.

"Now, we wait," Sally said, again wiping her hands.

41

The kitchen was beginning to smell good.

When the golden hoecakes were done, Sally moved them onto a larger *sahani*.

"You know when de edges get golden brown an crispy. Dat's when dey done."

When everything was cooked, Sally put it all together on a tray and called for Suzy. She picked up the tray and was gone as quickly as she'd come.

Sukey had survived her first new cooking lesson.

* * * *

Master James liked more than Sukey's hoecakes.

The first attack happened late at night. Sukey was sound asleep when he stumbled into the cabin and jumped upon her. She screamed, but no one in the cabin moved to help, everyone pretending to sleep.

"Don't you worry, pretty girl," Master James said afterwards. "Nobody else will bother you. You belong to me."

In the morning, Esther gave Sukey a soft hug.

"Baby chile, I knows. We all knows. It happen all de time . . . all de time."

Sukey put her head on Esther's chest and sobbed. She did not know the meaning of the words, but the sound gave her comfort.

* * * *

Aunt Sally took Sukey by the hand and headed for the hearth.

"De mos impohtan lesson I could evah learn you is takin good care of de cast iron pots. Chile, take keer dese pots wit you life! You take keer of dem, dey'll last forevah."

Sukey already knew Aunt Sally always cleaned the cast iron pots quickly after cooking and kept them seasoned with grease.

"I kin hear my mama speak to me when I cook," Sally continued. "She speak to me from de pots. Dat's why I take such good keer of dem pots cause it de only way I stay kinekted to her. If'n you doan take keer of yo pots, dey might take up legs an run away."

Sukey didn't catch all the words, but she understood the lesson.

* * * *

Aunt Sally pointed at a bunch of plump and sturdy tomatoes.

"To-maters."

Sally sliced the first one and placed it on a saucer. She grabbed the next one and put it in Sukey's hand.

"To-maters."

She then handed Sukey her sharp knife and motioned for her to follow suit.

"To-maters."

"To-maters," Sukey repeated as she picked up the knife. "Nyanya."

"Knife," corrected Sally. "Your nyanya is my knife. Now cut dese here to-maters."

Sukey put the knife into the soft flesh of the vegetable, but also into her finger. She winced and put her finger in her mouth to soothe the pain. Sally grabbed the pitcher from the counter, quickly pouring cool water on the cut finger.

"Dis chile doan even know how to slice maters without half-killin herself," she scolded. "How you sposed to help me?"

Sukey was heartbroken. Just when she was beginning to earn Aunt Sally's trust, she had failed with the *nyanya*.

Aunt Sally took a deep breath and wrapped Sukey's finger. She reached for another tomato, holding it in her hand.

"To-maters. Red to-maters."

"Red," she said again and turned Sukey toward the fire. "Red, fire is red."

"Hiyo imeumiza," Sukey flinched.

"Chile, I doan know what you sayin, but the Lawd spect us to forgive others. I guess I can forgive you too. You ain't hurt nobody but yoself. Come on here; let's finish lunch."

Sukey grabbed the *nyanya* and *kisu* and started cutting the most perfect slices she could. She followed Sally's pattern and arranged them on the *sahani* with the ones she cut before.

"Oh, looka you," Aunt Sally purred with satisfaction. The lessons continued, Sukey quickly becoming fluent in the most important words—fire, supper, cook, pot, water, food. She got the same instruction from the ladies in the cabin—sun, bed, sleep, smile, work . . .

As spring approached, Sukey not only knew a lot of words, but was beginning to string them together.

Aunt Sally, yo' is de bes' cook.

She may have been quickly learning this second lan-

44

guage but vowed she would never forget her own.

Wale ambao ni katika moja kuhusu chakula ni katika moja katika maisha.

Aunt Sally laughed. "What yo talkin bout chile? Speak Anglish."

If Sukey had a better grasp of *Anglish*, she would have said, "those who are at one regarding food are at one in life."

-6-

S ukey woke up to the sound of the bell clanging in the wind. She had slept soundly—probably the best since she had been stolen away from Goga—and it surprised her. The heat from the previous night had died down and a faint breeze wafted through the cabin.

Sukey was glad the door had been left open. The smells that lingered in the cabin after the field workers came back in the evening were pungent. It would take more than a few water buckets to wash away the stink of the day's work.

She had been working with Aunt Sally for at least six months, her respect continuing to grow. The same for Sally, who had finally warmed up to Sukey being her *mwanafunzi*. But Sukey had become more than a trainee; she was Aunt Sally's shadow. From sprinkling the seasonings to counting the number of times her spoon stirred in a bowl, she tried to do everything exactly like Sally. Thankfully, it was now a lot less stressful than it had been at the beginning. And it helped that Sukey had finally picked up the language.

"You sho is smart, Sukey. Is like you known Anglish all yo life."

Sukey acted as if she had not heard Sally's compliment, her African soul still fighting, still wishing.

* * * *

Sukey momentarily processed where she was and what she had lost, a recurring thought she'd faced time and again.

When I become propahty? I doan recall givin nobody de okay to rule ovah me.

* * * *

That first summer was unbearably hot. The breeze did not blow like it did in Goga. The heat just sat there. There was no escape. The corn had dried up, near burnt in a lightning storm.

Vittles were limited, served first to the white people with little left for the workers. The vegetables looked as spindly and sick as the animals. There were days when Sally didn't know what to fix. Sukey asked what they would do if the food ran out, but Sally had no answer.

"We do what we gots to do," she said. "An den wait for de rain."

Since work in the field had dried up, Sukey figured Master James would have taken it easy on everyone. No way.

Mastah mad an cruel all de time. Sun up ta sun down, he gots erebody buildin somethin up or tearin somethin down. Even de hoecakes doan sweeten him up.

One hot and humid day, for no apparent reason, Master James took the whip to Absalom. Furious at what she

47

saw, Sukey had worked up the gumption to confront Master James. Aunt Sally grabbed her arm and pulled her backward.

"Sukey, de blood done boil up in yo face. You looks like you need to make some bread."

"Aunt Sally, I doan feel like makin no bread," Sukey huffed, slamming down her cooking spoon.

Sally yanked Sukey again.

"We gonna stir all de fixins together into a ball," said Sally, calmly. "Den we gonna plop dat dough on the table and knead. You know my bakin bread rule."

Sukey nodded her head, positive she would hear it again.

"De mo you knead de bettah de bread."

Aunt Sally put her hand on Sukey's shoulder.

"Chile, in times like dis, you take all dat mad an you put it into de dough. You jes knead an keep yo mouf shut. Mastah always praise me when I knead a long time. He say he can tell de diffrence. Little do he know, I'm puttin my hate on him in de bread."

Sukey kneaded that dough to perfection.

* * * *

Later that week, the white overseers couldn't find Absalom when they rousted everybody for breakfast. His pallet was empty.

"Must have run off sometime in the night," said Master James. "Who here knows where he is?"

There was no answer, of course, although nobody seemed surprised.

"Well, he ain't gonna get far," James growled.

Sukey had heard Absalom mumbling about being sick of Master James' mistreatment and how nobody had the right to own him. She also wanted to run. But where would she go? She didn't even know where she was. She had heard talk of Freedom Land up north, but where was that?

Absalom was gone a full two days before they dragged him back, kicking and spitting. Once again, Master James called the plantation together to witness the punishment. He announced that in addition to disappearing from the plantation, Absalom had been caught trying to steal a chicken from a nearby farm.

"I'm guessing you was hungry, huh, Absalom? Sally's food wasn't good enough for you?" He paused for a second. "Heat the brand up good, Thomas. We gonna have to mark this nigra a runaway."

Grinning, Overseer Thomas was already at the firepit, blowing on the coals.

"Hold on there, Absalom," he laughed. "Gotta make this blaze extra hot."

The brand glowed a deep orange as Thomas displayed it to the crowd. The other white men tied Absalom's hands behind him and held his lower jaw tightly from behind so he couldn't move his face. Real quick-like, Master Thomas thrust the fiery R brand onto Absalom's face just near his left eye.

Absalom screamed. Even Master James cried aloud. Although Sukey looked away, her first thought was that Absalom was being blinded.

"Oh, did that hurt?" said Master James. "You don't even know the level of hurt awaitin' you, boy. Stealing from good white folk. Tie him up."

The white men tied Absalom to the whipping post, tearing off his shirt to reveal the unhealed scabs from his last beating.

Master James stepped in front of Thomas, whip in hand.

"The punishment for this crime is forty lashes save one," said James, "and I'm gonna be sure you receive every single one."

Master Shields counted aloud with each swing. By lash five, Absalom's back ran with blood. If he weren't tied to the post, it's doubtful he would have been able to stand the entire thrashing. Sukey almost blacked out from watching.

When he finished, James motioned Thomas to untie Absalom, who fell to the ground looking practically dead. Adding to the horror, Thomas grabbed Absalom and sat him up while James wrapped an iron collar around his neck. Not only did the collar look heavy, it had long stems extending from it.

"You try to run now, boy, this little necklace will hang you up in the brush." James stopped for a minute and squinted at Absalom. "Matter of fact, you might need a little more."

Thomas handed James some large bells.

"We call these shackle bells," James whispered to Absalom. "Now I can hear every move you make!"

Sukey felt completely undone at her master's savagery, although she did not confront him. Nor did she feel like making bread.

When she looked in on Absalom later that evening, Sukey was both fearful and sickened. Suzy had laid wet rags on his back to soothe the pain, but pools of blood had gathered beneath the cloth. Each time she tried to re-wet the rags, she pulled the skin that had dried and reopened the wounds. Absalom tried to readjust his body to get away from the pain, but the stems from the collar prevented him from moving. Sukey felt helpless but knew what she had to do.

Aunt Sally had taught her how to cook up salves and remedies for times such as these.

"White folks go to doctors," Sally told Sukey. "All we have is what the Good Lawd gave us."

Sukey gently rubbed honey on Absalom's wounds.

* * * *

Sukey had been an excellent student. During the winter, Sally had taught Sukey how to make a spring tonic to prevent illness and energize the children. On the first sunny day after winter, Sally got all the children lined up for a heaping spoonful.

"It'll keep dem right through the spring thaw. No sickness here. Ain't nobody got time fo dat!"

Sally had the healing touch. First, she would try to feed the ailment out of a patient. If that didn't work, she had some tea or ointment that could cure anyone. Sally swore by the remedy of drinking pot liquor, the liquid left in the pot after cooking greens. For everyday pains, she'd send Sukey outside to find some special weeds by the barn. If Sukey returned with the correct weed, Sally would always say, "Ah, yes, deres your looker," and then throw it into a pot of boiling water to steep.

Sally said a little lion's tongue tea could knock the pain right out of a toothache or a bout with the rheumatism. When the children had the croup and had trouble breathing, she'd fix them up some "Jewsalem oak" tea. To avoid getting sick at all, she always wore a necklace of devil's dung on her chest. She said it stunk so bad it kept the other sicknesses away. It must have worked. Aunt Sally was always cooking. Sukey had never even seen her cough.

Sally had a collection of proven remedies. For asthma, she would use tea made of chestnut leaves. Sally would boil poke roots and add sugar to make a syrup. She used horehound for colds, adding either brown sugar or whiskey. For fever, she went with peach tree leaves. And for an upset stomach, she would crush the peach tree leaves, pour water over them, and wouldn't let the sick person drink anything else until they were better.

* * * *

Early one morning, Master James sent for Sukey.

"Sukey, you and Jasper go on down to Millers' Store and pick up some supplies. Here, write down a list."

"A list, Mastah? What dat?"

"Lord, silly me. You don't know how to write. I'll just tell you the things to tell Mrs. Miller we need. You think you can remember?"

"Yes, Mastah. I'll member good."

While Jasper went to hitch up the wagon, Master Shields recited a bunch of items he expected to be purchased.

"You know, Sukey, just tell Mrs. Miller we need the same supplies as last time and to include some blankets," he said. "And tell her to add it to my bill at the end of the month. I'll write your passes."

He went into the parlor and came back with the papers. "Here's one for you and one for Jasper. Don't lose them."

Just then, Jasper pulled up with the wagon.

"Let me help you in, Miss Sukey." As she climbed up, Jasper pushed her from behind. "I's sorry for touchin you like that, Miss Sukey."

"Oh, that's alright, Jaspah. You was jes helpin."

The ride into town was bumpy, but Sukey was happy to be off the plantation. She took in a big sniff of the fresh air and watched the birds flying in the air. It was peaceful and quiet. Sukey had never really been alone with Jasper and neither said a word. After a while, the silence felt awkward.

"Jaspah," Sukey finally said, "Months ago, de day I got here, you was bein brung back to the plantation. I heared you tried to run away. Where was you going?"

"I was goin to Freedom Land up north."

"Where dis Freedom Land; how you know how to get dere?"

"I doan know, but I gots to find it. I'm not fo dis slavin life. I'm gonna run agin. I'll nevah stop tryin to get my freedom."

"But las time, Mastah whoop you so hard, you jes bout died. Ain't you fraid of dyin?

"Death be bettah dan bein a slave. If'n he kill me; let him kill me. Either way, I be free!"

Jasper smiled and began to hum.

"Jaspah, what dat song you hummin? It sound nice."

"It jes a song bout freedom. Wanna hear?"

Jasper belted out a few bars.

> "Oh Freedom Oh freedom
> No mo chains, no mo whips,
> No mo' massa to please.
> I'm gonna be wit my Jesus de King."

Sukey listened intently, impressed that he sang with such power.

As they pulled up to the store, Sukey looked at Jasper and whispered, "How you gon know the right time to try again?"

Jasper lowered his eyes and looked over both shoulders before answering her.

"When de wind blows jes right, I gonna know."

Sukey nodded but couldn't help thinking that Jasper's plan was far from foolproof.

"Okay, let's go get Massah's supplies," said Jasper. "We doan keep him waitin."

Jasper helped Sukey descend the wagon and they walked into the doorway of the Millers' store. Her jaw dropped open when she saw the inside.

She grabbed Jasper's arm and pulled him close.

"Dis place so big, Jaspah. So many things. What us gon do here?"

"Dis be where people come to shop, to buy things dey need."

"Jasper," a white man appeared from behind the counter, "I haven't seen you in ages."

"It be a month a Sundays, Mistah Millah." He paused before continuing. "Massa Shields sent us down here to fetch his usual ordah fo de season. He say to tell Missus Miller to put it on his bill."

"Of course, James Shields' credit is good here. Whatever he needs."

Jasper and Mr. Miller scurried about filling sacks and crates with the items Master James wanted—coffee, tea, spices, rice, beans, flour, sugar, salt, cornmeal, crackers, molasses, kerosene.

Mr. Miller went in the back and got some farm tools for Jasper to carry out to the wagon as well.

"What you need, gal?" The sudden appearance of an older white women startled Sukey.

"B-b-b-blankets!"

As the lady walked away, Sukey noticed that her large dress seemed like it was bouncing in the breeze.

Sukey was not sure how many blankets Master Shields needed, but Mrs. Miller dumped a stack of them in her arms. They were heavy and felt scratchy against her face. Barely balanced, Sukey made her way back to the wagon. Jasper took the load from her and started packing them away.

"Uh oh," he said, "deres a stain on dis here blanket. We can't take dis back to Massa. He be mad fo sho. I'll take it back in and show Missus Millah and ask her for a new one. You wait right here. I'll be right back."

Sukey would never see Jasper again.

-7-

"Nisaidie! Nisaidie!" Sukey feared so much she forgot the prohibition against her native language. "Master! Oh, hep me! Hep me, Master!" Without Jasper, Sukey had driven the wagon back to the plantation by herself. Thankfully, the horses seemed to know the way. The closer they got to the estate, the faster the horses galloped. Seeing Sukey struggling to stay seated as the horses bounced her down the lane, Malachi had jumped onto the wagon and pulled the reins.

"Malachi, thank you! I was so scared! Dey jes took off!"

Master Shields ran toward the wagon, fuming.

"What in the hell is going on out here? Sukey, why are you driving by yourself? Where's Jasper?"

Sukey felt overwhelmed by a sudden sense of shame and embarrassment, though she didn't know why. She lowered her head, expecting the worst.

"I doan know, Mastah. He nevah came out de Millah stow."

"Whatchu mean he never came out of the Millers? Where'd he go?"

"I doan know, Mastah."

Although they had talked about it, Sukey never thought

Jasper would run away *today*, much less leave her to face Master Shields' wrath alone.

"He nevah come back. Dere was a stain on one of de blankets and he say he was goin back in to talk to Missus Miller. He tol me to wait for him in de wagon, and I did jes that."

"Liar!" Master slapped her face hard. "You are protecting him! You helped him set this up!"

"I promise, Mastah, I didn't know nothin about dis."

Master Shields turned to his second in command.

"Thomas, get the dogs and some of the men. We're going hunting."

Thomas and a few white men returned five minutes later, the dogs already barking and howling.

"Let's get a move on. He's got a couple hours lead, but we'll catch him. When we see him, shoot on sight. Don't kill him, just wound him. I got big plans for Jasper. Sukey, I'll deal with you when I get back."

Sukey stood frozen by the prospect of what was to come later. Aunt Sally took her hand and led her to the kitchen as a few of the workers carried the parcels in from the wagon. Peace, a young slave girl who had been tending the garden, was called into the kitchen to help.

"Sukey, jes sit dere an relax," Sally said in her calming voice. "Peace gonna help put de stuff away. Yous had a hahd day."

Peace didn't want to get in Sally's way, but just the same, didn't want to put anything in the wrong place. For her part, Sally didn't miss a step in the process, seeming to delight in barking out orders.

"Put dem beans up on dat shef ovah dere, Peace. We

ain't need dem right away today. Gimme dat rice. Fill dis pot wid cold watah and put it on to boil."

After several minutes, Sally turned to Sukey.

"Sukey, you been sittin long enuff. Bettah you be busy. C'mon ovah heah and I'll learn you how to make a pork pie that'll put de blacksmith's anvils on Mastah's eyelids. Heah's what you gotta do. Skin six or so taters and slice em thin. Den chop up one onion. Buttah dat dere dish an place one layer of dem taters on the bottom and sprinkle em wit onions. Den alls you gots to do is spread on a layer of cold roast pork and cover dat wit milk."

Sukey immediately started slicing and chopping.

"Den we gonna put all dat on the coals," added Aunt Sally. "It'll bake up nice an thick-like in a lil while."

By the time Master Shields dragged the dogs and horses into the barn, Aunt Sally had a spread laid out on the table.

"That boy must have had help. We couldn't find hide nor hair of him. We walked through the river; mud up to our knees. The dogs never even picked up his scent. Somebody is hiding him, but he ain't gonna get away. I'll find him." Screaming now, he said, "You hear that, Jasper? You ain't escaping from me! I'll find you!"

Aunt Sally interrupted, "Master, why doan you come on an sit down and get yoself sumpin ta eat. You must be stahvin. Heah, have some of dis heah pork pie. I made you some of dat mint tea you like to wash it all down. An I made you some apple pan dowdy fo dessert. C'mon an set a spell. Let's stop all this fussin bout some runaway slave."

"Sukey, you sure he ain't said nothing to you about running away?"

"Naw suh, Mastah, suh. We was jes singin and talkin bout how we wanna make it to heaven someday. Dat's it. I promise."

"Heaven, huh? That better be all y'all talked about. Aunt Sally, what else you got sweet? I am famished!"

"Well, I got some sorghum cake. Let me cut you a big slice. I baked it up special cause I knowed you be hungry. I brewed you up a pot a coffee too. Hopin it doan keep you awake none."

"Oh, don't you worry about that. I'm dog tired. Once my head hits the pillow, I'll be gone."

You go, Mastah, and doan evah come back.

-8-

"Sukey!"

Malachi's call awakened Yuda from her deep sleep. "Come quick, it's Aunt Sally! She ailin somethin awful!"

Sukey and Malachi ran as fast as they could to Aunt Sally's quarters. The older woman had been having difficulty walking of late. This morning, it looked like the left side of her face was sliding down toward her neck, like butter when it hits the hot skillet. Her voice sounded strange, her words slurring together.

She looked at Sukey and tried to straighten her stance.

"Sukey, whatchu doin heah? Who takin care of Mastah's biscuits?"

With that, she drifted back to sleep. For a moment, Sukey feared Aunt Sally had died, but her stomach still lifted with each laboring breath.

Roused awake by all the commotion, Master James came to Sally's bedside and took one look.

"Well, looks like Aunt Sally has made it to the end," he said in a matter of fact tone. "She's not long for this world."

Dat's cold. Why not jes march in heah and say, "Well, Aunt Sally's a goner, y'all."

Aunt Sally never got out of her bed again.

For many years, Sukey would remember the day they carried Sally's body out to be buried. Malachi and some of the other menfolk had dug out a hole for her. They laid her body to rest and the old slave preacher began to talk.

He jes makin a bunch a noise ovah her.

As the preacher took a step back, Aunt Esther, with her beautiful voice, started singing a song.

> Good-bye, my sistah, good-bye, hallelujah!
> Good-bye, sistah Sally, good-bye, hallelujah!
> Goin home, hallelujah!
> Jesus call me, hallelujah!
> Lingah no longah, hallelujah!
> Tarry no longah, hallelujah!"

Most of the other mourners joined in the singing and shared their sad goodbyes. Aunt Sally was barely cold in the ground before Master James called everyone back to work.

"Ain't no use in sitting around, old Sally ain't coming back."

He shooed his hand and turned to Sukey.

"Sukey, you run the kitchen now. Aunt Sally done trained you well. How bout you fix me up some of them good hoecakes and sliced tomatahs in her honor?"

"Yes, Mastah."

Sukey entered the kitchen that day in reverence as she reflected on the days and nights she'd spent with Aunt Sally mixing, cooking, and talking. So strange to be without her. Sukey would make Master's hoecakes in Aunt Sally's memory. She would make them the best she could.

That first few weeks after Sally passed away, Sukey felt overwhelmed as she prepared meals for the white household and the entire plantation, close to forty people. Kitchen work was especially hard because the menfolk had to be in the fields by sunrise, what Sally used to call "caint see time." They had already worked for several hours before Sukey called them for breakfast. That's when she got to work on the white folks' breakfast.

Aunt Sally always say to keep de Mastah "fed up good."

Master Shields assigned Aunt Esther to help in the kitchen until Sukey got her footing. Aunt Sally had trusted Esther.

Aunt Sally jes doan wan anybody in her kitchen.

Strange, but whenever Sukey was in the kitchen, she felt Aunt Sally's presence. If she sprinkled salt or some spice in a dish, she could hear Sally suck her teeth and say, "Chile, whatchu doin? I didn't teach you like dat. Doan make me come back dere!"

Sukey expected Aunt Sally to appear at any moment.

"Aunt Esther, do you evah feel Aunt Sally's ghost roamin round heah?"

"Lawd yes, she up dere thinkin dis still her kitchen."

Later that afternoon, when Esther had gone to check on the garden, Sukey gathered her voice and yelled aloud, "Listen, old haint, I aims to do things my way now and you should stop botherin me and get to livin in the aftahlife and leave the cookin to me."

Sally's spirit never bothered Sukey again.

-9-

Sukey was carrying vegetables from the garden when Master James stopped her. She sensed anger.

"Sukey, how long you been here?"

"Doan know, Mastah, long time."

"Well, it was almost 1808 when I bought you, so I've been servicing you pretty regular for about five years. And you haven't produced not one child for me. You dry or something?"

"Doan know, Mastah. I's sorry yo upset."

"I paid a lot of money for you . . . and put in a lot of trouble. So, I expect some results."

Master James would soon be rewarded.

* * * *

It was a beautiful day in May, the Shields plantation ripe with new growth. Sukey's friends kept telling her she was close to giving birth, but she was not quite ready.

Sukey had started the day as usual, up early to make breakfast for everybody, when she felt a sharp pain in her back. Sukey didn't think too much about it, but after a while the pain grew so great that it took her breath away.

She winced and sucked her teeth loud. From outside the kitchen door, young Patience stopped shucking corn and rushed to her side.

"Miss Sukey, you feelin awwrite?"

"I's fine. Jes feelin pains real strong."

Moments later, Sukey lay in a ball on the floor, a tiny puddle on the ground underneath her. Patience thought Sukey had peed herself.

"Patience, get de nuhse! I doan feel good."

"I caint leave you lone, Miss Sukey!" Her fear and concern only increased Sukey's.

"Go get Miss Jane, now! Owww!"

Within the hour, Sukey had screamed so much her throat hurt. She pictured Master James for a moment but drove the vision out of her mind with a powerful push. She also squeezed Miss Jane's hand so hard that the plantation midwife momentarily worried her fingers might be broken.

Suddenly, after a tremendous shot of pain, a strong baby boy popped out. Miss Jane slapped him on his butt; his cry was loud and strong.

I caint believe I's somebody's mama.

Master James came into the kitchen when Sukey's screams had finally stopped. He smiled and didn't mind boasting he had a new slave born on his property.

Barely paying attention to Master James, Miss Jane softly stroked Sukey's hair.

"Miss Sukey, what ya gonna name dis hansum boy?" Miss Jane asked.

That was easy. Sukey would name him Ayinde, a strong African name meaning "praise."

Master Shields interrupted.

"Ain't it my right to name my property?" he declared emphatically. "We will call him Sam; that's a good American name."

Ayinde. Master say Sam be his boy. He ain't none a his! He mine!

Ayinde. Dat be our secret, beautiful chile.

-10-

"Alas, another summer of this dreadful heat," Sukey heard James lament to Timothy as she worked the garden. "We're barely holding on as it is."

Sukey stopped working to wipe the sweat from her brow and fan herself. It had not rained for quite a long time and the garden grew pitifully. Sukey took pride in the usual colors of fruits, vegetables, and flowers but now nothing was vibrant. Barely anything had grown this year, especially the slaves' bellies. Sukey was glad Sam still sucked on her breasts for food. For sure, he would have starved by now.

Neither the heat nor the fact that she had a baby had not stopped Master James from his late-night visits. Just before harvest, Sukey realized she was once again pregnant.

Several times during that summer of 1815, Sukey had overheard Master Shields talking to his wife about their bills and creditors.

"If this drought continues, I don't know what we're going to do," Sukey heard him say. "We need relief. We need rain!"

But it didn't rain. In fact, things turned so dry fires broke out on the plantation. Despite Shields' charge to the slaves to carry buckets of water from the well to douse the flames, they still lost quite a bit of farm grounds. The earth charred from the scorching.

To make up for his losses, Shields started selling off some of his assets, including people. He had not been "to market" for a long time. He loaded up the cart with many of the workers, including Patience, Peace, and Miss Jane. He even took Absalom.

Sukey tearfully watched her friends being loaded onto the master's wagon. He was taking the only family she'd known, except for her baby, since her village had been stolen from her. She was heartbroken, cringing at the thought of her friends going to market and what might become of them. If Master Shields didn't like to eat so much, Sukey realized she probably would have been on the wagon too.

If only it would have rained.

Miss Jane, who had doctored Sukey during birth, had been on this plantation for almost fifty years. She'd been born here and gifted to Master James when he was a mere child. Without warning, she was now being ripped from her home. Say what you want, this was her home. The crags in Miss Jane's face deepened as she wiped crying eyes with her dress. The dress looked eerily bland to Sukey, as if the color had drained out to match Jane's face. Eyes sunken into her skull, she appeared somehow old and frail.

Absalom glared from the wagon. He hated the plantation, hated Master Shields, hated Thomas. Sukey did not care for Absalom, but it was still hard to see him taken away. The scuttlebutt suggested Absalom would probably be sold deeper south. That R on his face—for *Runaway*—promised him a hard life. No good or kind master would buy and treat him well. That scar would surely ruin his life.

Peace was true to her name. Her empathetic demeanor was a spiritual gift to their enslaved family. It was as if Peace always had a song in her heart, a voice that would warm the night with words to welcome the good side of life. And she was wonderful with Sam, her antics keeping him joyful in play.

When Sukey was somber—and that was often—Peace could ease the pain.

"Sukey, you is so pretty, speshly when you smile." Peace had said that more than once, but now her tears tore through Sukey's soul.

And Patience, although quiet and subdued, was a great helper in the garden and around the kitchen. She carried well water, dumped ashes from the fireplace, even swept off the porch when the wind had blown dust from the garden.

"Patience, you got a real servant's heart," Master Shields had said one day.

Now he was selling her to who knows who?

Like a child, Sukey's arms involuntarily and independently reached out to touch her friends one last time. She wanted to hug and hold each one of them for a long, long time. She stood that way until she couldn't see the cart anymore.

Sukey continued to cry, wondering if she would ever see them again.

-11-

T he cabin was down to Sukey, Esther, and Sam, who had just turned one. In fact, the entire plantation was a skeleton of what it once had been, only twelve slaves total. Plus, the overseers were gone, Thomas the last to leave, rumor circulating he had signed to be a slave catcher.

In March of 1816, Sukey gave birth to her second son. His secret name would be Chaminuka, "An Exalted King." Master James named him George after the first president of the United States.

Sam, who had just learned to walk, immediately loved George. Master Shields, as he had done with Sam, gave not even a hint that he was the father, that these children might be special to him.

"So happy to have another slave," he again bragged.

Sukey could not fathom such nonsense.

I love dese chillen even though theys half-white. How could anyone be so cold to dey own blood?

The bare cabin seemed energized with new life. While nursing Chaminuka, Sukey remembered a time in Africa she had hid in the bushes to witness a mother giraffe giving birth.

With brown diamond-shaped spots speckling her tan fur, the mother giraffe towered over the tallest bush on the savannah. Yuda watched as a quick flick of the giraffe's tail revealed two long legs sticking out from her rear end.

The mother giraffe swung her long neck around and began to lick at the fluid covering her calf's legs. Small brown pellets fell from her rump. She was giving birth and *kusisimua* at the same time! As she pushed the calf out, at least a couple of hundred little balls also dropped down. Yuda looked closer at the legs, and sure enough, a little face started to appear. Legs, a face, and *kujisaidia* all at once! It looked like the mother's insides were coming out as the baby began to slide. Young Yuda realized giving birth was not an easy process. The thin legs simply dangled in the air and, at first, the calf looked dead. But the mother relentlessly pushed and tightened her muscles as the slimy baby slid further down. Suddenly, a gush of liquid released and the calf fell to the ground with a thud. The baby's introduction to the world was a six-foot fall from its mother.

Ouch! Welcome to Goga, little twiga!

After a moment, the mother giraffe lowered her head and, with her long purplish tongue, licked the slime from her baby.

Sukey's own babies had been covered in a similar slime, but she sure was glad not to have to lick them clean.

* * * *

One warm evening in late summer, as Malachi and Esther watched the baby and played with Sam, Sukey

70

took a walk through the woods that touched the edge of the plantation. The sky was turning a dark, musty blue, the stars already prominent.

As she approached a small stream, her thoughts drifted home. She pictured the many ceremonies of her culture—births, deaths, marriages—and how the drums would sound a chorus of emotion.

Within her mind, Sukey began to hear those drums . . . and she became lost in their rhythm. She danced and swayed and jumped, moving to the sound of the pumpkin djembe.

I am Yuda and Goga is my home.

She remembered when Dinka presented her with a broken-open coconut that he had climbed a tree to obtain. Although they were children, this was his way of expressing his love for her. Yuda remembered that his eyes twinkled as he bowed before her. And the drums of the village celebrated their promise to each other. A sad twinge filled her heart, their life together lost.

But the drums Yuda heard in her head were growing louder. To be home. To be in the place of her birth. To live in Goga's womb. In her mind, Yuda could see the huts of her village, the rolling hills filled with trees, and she now danced underneath the waterfalls. She was alive and a deep spiritual growl purred within her, a scream that had to be released.

She called to her home.

"Goga, nyumbani na asili yangu nchi, jinsi I kwa muda mrefu kwa wewe! damu yangu majipu kama nadhani kuhusu wewe."

Yuda told Goga how she longed to see her, how her

blood boiled without her.

"Ninataka kwenda nyumbani! Nataka kuwa huru! Nataka kuwa huru! Nataka kuwa huru!" she screamed. "I want to be free!"

Each syllable voiced made her angrier. Tears fell down her face, but the drums kept talking, kept calling to her . . . and she would answer.

"I member you, Goga! You what nurshed me at your supple teat, fed me, gave me life. You nevah made me a beas of buhden. You let me roam free, I nevah guess at who I am when I's was wid you. I's a whole puhson. You honah my dark skin, my flesh baked in yo ambah sun. And now, I slave at de fires of dese white people who stole me away from you. Dey doan see you in me. Dey see an animal. Mimi si mnyama. I's not an animal. I want out of this cage. Nataka kuwa huru!"

Master's booming voice crushed the moment.

"What in the hell is going on here?" he yelled.

Yuda was wrenched from her trance, the sound of drums gone. Once again, a white man had stolen Goga from her.

"What are you doing here, Sukey? Did I give permission for a party? I recall telling you I didn't want that African talk here! And now I could hear it from the house. What is this Goga you keep screaming about?"

"Dat is my home, Mastah. I miss it so much."

"Your home? This is your home. Virginia! You live here on my plantation. I don't want to hear anything about Africa on my land again. If I hear it one more time, there will be hell to pay!"

A tear welled in the corner of Sukey's eye and dropped heavily to her bosom. The single tear unleashed a flood from her eyes. She tasted the salty liquid as it went over her lips. Her nose dripped and mixed in with her tears. She sucked inward and wiped her face with her sleeve.

"Cut this insanity," Master James snapped. "Get back to your cabin and stay there until breakfast."

* * * *

Sukey prepared the morning meal in silence. Her spirits heavy, she completed her chores in a stupor. Afterwards, she slumped against a wall and slid down until her bottom rested on the floor. She could hear a tense conversation in the parlor.

"James, what are we going to do? You sold off most of the slaves and we're still struggling. They're going to take our house away."

"How many times are we going to talk about this, Amelia?" he snapped. "I know how bad it is. I don't know what else to do!"

Sukey heard a fist pound the table.

"Settle down, James. I just think we need a plan."

"We have twelve slaves and can't afford to feed them," he said. "I have a letter from a possible buyer in Kentucky. He is willing to pay a strong price. I can't pass up this deal. Sell the slaves and hopefully some of the land, then start over."

"The land? The slaves? A buyer?"

"It's our only hope, Amelia."

"Wait, not all the slaves. You're not talking about Sukey. We can't lose Sukey! What are we going to do without a cook?"

Sukey heard James stand up and walk out. She grinned at the prospect of getting away from Master Shields.

* * * *

Several months later, in late October, Sukey was in the garden when a white man approached on horseback.

James came out of the house, rifle in hand.

"Can I help you, sir?"

"Yes, I'm looking for James Shields."

"You found him."

"I am Henry Rutherford, a broker out of Mississippi. I was passing through headed for Leesburg and heard you might have some stock for sale."

"You heard right, but I am afraid I already have a letter of intent from a Kentucky buyer."

"Mind to tell me his offer?"

"I would enjoy discussing the current market, Mr. Rutherford. Perhaps you can stay for supper. We have a guest room should you care to get back on the road in the morning."

"That's most kind of you. I would very much enjoy a rest from travel."

As he dismounted, Henry eyed Sukey.

"Oh, this is Sukey, our cook," said James. "You are going to be in for quite a treat."

"I hope so." Henry tipped his hat to Sukey.

Later, after she had finished cleaning the kitchen, Sukey stepped out into the twilight. From behind, someone grabbed her by the chest and neck, forcibly pulling her around. It was the slave broker, his hand now covering her mouth and the other yanking at her dress.

"I'm still hungry, Miss Sukey."

She said nothing. She knew the routine.

* * * *

A few days after the slave broker came and went, James told Sukey to prepare a feast for about five or six guests who would be arriving the next day.

"I know there's not much," he said, "but find something. They'll stay for a couple of days."

No food for the workers, but let's white folks have a party.

Sure enough, a group of six men—three on horseback— arrived with three wagons. James and Amelia greeted the strangers at the door.

"Y'all must be tired from such a long trip," said James. "Which of you is Colonel Bowman?"

"That would be me," said one of the men on horseback, the oldest in the group.

"Wonderful to meet you, sir. Please, everyone, c'mon in."

With all the extra mouths to feed, Sukey had a tough time working and finding a moment to catch the gossip. As close as she could figure, this Colonel Bowman was a war hero, explorer, and businessman who owned 8,000 acres of land in Kentucky. She knew why their wagons were empty.

The next afternoon, James came down to the kitchen.

"Sukey, I have sold you, your children, and the rest of the slaves to Colonel Bowman. I'm telling you first and will be calling everyone together shortly to give them the news. Y'all will be leaving in the morning."

Sukey was stunned at the matter-of-fact manner of his words. She decided to twist his moral conscience.

"No, Mastah, please doan sell us off. You said this here our home. What us gon do?"

"Now, Sukey. This is a done deal. You are going to Kentucky with a fine upstanding citizen. He'll take care of you and the boys."

Mastah doan care if we safe. He jes happy to get de money.

This plantation was no Goga, still it was the only home she had known in this awful country. Once again, a white man was taking it all away.

-12-

The foreboding sky bespoke the change ahead. The Indian summer had lasted into early November, the darkness of the sky perhaps signaling the possibility of rain. Sukey thought it funny that for all of Master James' wishing and praying for rain, it would finally arrive as they were leaving.

Colonel Bowman had packed his wagons with plenty of supplies, appearing they would be traveling a great distance. Sukey had fried several chickens, enough to feed the three wagons of slaves and Bowman's helpers. She also had hidden several tomatoes in her apron pockets, planning to keep them for herself and her boys. So little of her life was just for her; at the very least, she was owed a couple of meager tomatoes.

She kept George close by and nursed him at her breast when he cried. He didn't cry much. He seemed to enjoy the open road and the steady gallop of the horses. In the silence of the journey, Sukey longed to take her children home to Goga. She once again imagined how they would have run as they chased the playful monkeys that stole fruit from the huts. She giggled at the thought.

When the horses needed to rest, Colonel Bowman

called for the wagons to stop and the workmen pitched
tents for the night. Ordered to pick kindling and search
for firewood, Sukey laid the boys under one of the burlap shelters and began her chores. Tending the fires was
hardly an unfamiliar task. As the sun went down, Sukey
nestled both her babies near her, trying not to fret about a
new master's physical intentions. To settle her mind, she
quietly sang to the boys.

> "Jua pia limeweka,
> Usingizi usingizi usingizi,
> Ndege zote wamelala,
> Usingizi usingizi usingizi."

A tear fell from Yuda's chin onto George's cheek.
"My mama sang that song to me when I was a young
girl," she whispered in his little ear.
When Master Bowman delivered her to Belle Grove
after two days and nights of wagon travel, Sukey was
amazed by the beauty of the plantation. From the back
of the wagon, her eyes lit upon the big house sitting back
beyond the road. Its four columns rose from the porch
like grand towers. She couldn't appreciate all its glory for
counting the number of windows.
I ain't cleanin' all dem windahs! I'm a cook.
Sukey was helped from the wagon by one of Colonel
Bowman's men, who methodically removed her chains
and shackles. Colonel Bowman tied his horse to the wagon
and handed Sukey her baby. Sam jumped into his arms.
Rubbing her wrists as she turned around, Sukey was
surprised that her friends were still in the three wagons.

"Malachi? Esther? Whatchall doin? C'mon down now."

"Sukey, Belle Grove is *your* new home," said Colonel Bowman. My cousin, Isaac, is in need of a good cook. I have sold you and your children to him. Everyone else is going to Kentucky to work at my plantation."

Confused, Sukey looked at her friends, then directed her eyes toward the ground.

"But Mastah Bowman, doan you need a cook?"

Bowman did not answer, instead turning to his men.

"Y'all get on now. Pick up the six new slaves in Harrisonburg and I'll catch up with you where we camped before in Clifton Forge, if not sooner."

Bowman untied his horse from the wagon.

"You know the way. See you soon."

Sukey noticed a man walking briskly from the mansion.

"Cousin Abraham, you old war horse. So good to see you."

"Isaac, I am so happy to be here. You look . . . almost ancient."

The two men laughed and hugged.

"Isaac, this is Sukey. She is a fantastic cook! According to the man I purchased her from, a Mr. Shields, she makes the best hoecakes in the world."

"Sukey, welcome to Belle Grove. I am the Reverend Major Isaac Hite."

"Pleased to meet you, suh." She bowed as she had seen other white women do when they met someone. She had overheard Missus Amelia tell her daughters to "kuhtsee" when they talked to a gentleman.

"And these must be your two boys."

"Yessuh. Dis is Sam and my baby is George."

"They are handsome boys, Sukey."

"Thank ya suh."

Dis man be-in way too nice.

Just then, a white woman approached.

"Ah, and this is your mistress," said Master Hite. "Everyone calls her Miss Ann. Love, I want you to meet Sukey, our new cook."

"Welcome, Sukey."

"Pleased to meet you, Miss Ann. An' dese are my two sons, Sam and George. Dey won't be no trouble. Dey's good boys."

"You'll be happy here," said Miss Ann. "Our slaves are just like family to us. And the Reverend Hite is a good and kind master."

Ann looked off to her left and gasped slightly.

"Hello Abraham, as I live and breathe!"

"Ann, it's been five years. Walker was a baby and little Ann must have been about six last I was here. And look at you, another baby."

"Yes, this is Hugh. The other kids are down at Cedar Creek with Nelly. They'll be back shortly. This is so exciting. How long can you stay?"

"Three days, if you'll have me," said Abraham. "It's a two-week trip to Bowman's Station and I really want to be home by Thanksgiving."

"Your letter mentioned you have more slaves to pick up in Harrisonburg?" asked Isaac.

"Yes, taking 15 back to Kentucky, in all . . . three wagons full. I plan to catch up with my crew around Clifton Forge."

"Well, we can settle our business after dinner," said

Isaac. "Thank you so much for purchasing Sukey and her boys. I can hardly wait to taste her cooking."

"Probably not tonight," inserted Ann. "But we do have a big dinner planned, Abraham, and our guest room awaits you."

Master Hite lifted Sam onto his hip.

"Sukey, you go on ahead inside with my wife and I'll see that your boys are watched by one of the girls over there on the lawn."

Sam was already eyeing the other kids at play, a few close to his age.

"Eliza," yelled Master Hite, "you and Fanny watch these two little ones."

Sam was already into the mix of children when Eliza took George from Sukey's arms.

"Dis baby so hansum."

"Eliza, this is Sukey, our new cook."

"Thank de Lawd, a real cook. I's so happy you is here."

Sukey hesitated at the idea of leaving her boys, but Miss Ann nudged her along into the house.

"We'll set you up in your own place in just a while," Ann told her.

Sukey felt a bit nervous about walking inside such a large dwelling. Part of her felt ashamed, but she didn't know why. The feeling stayed with her as they began a tour of the house, entering through a lower door. It felt odd to Sukey having the mistress leading the way.

Mebbe it be diffrent here at Belle Grove. Mebbe de Hites diffrent dan de Shields. Mastah James was jes mean. De Hites seem so kind.

Miss Ann smiled as she talked, as if she was showing the

area to a group of white ladies.

"To the right is the kitchen area" she said. "Inside there, you can access the pig room. That's where we bring the pigs in from outside through the door there and then slaughter and butcher them. Makes quite a big mess and smells awful, but we get the best hams and bacon."

She led Sukey into the kitchen.

"This is not the main cooking area. This is primarily the scullery. And this is Suzy. She's Truelove's daughter, who you will meet later. Suzy has been helping in the scullery while we get the cooking situation solved."

"Scullery, ma'am? What dat?"

"In the scullery, you will mainly clean the vegetables. The cooking takes place in the bigger kitchen. I will show you that area shortly."

Sukey felt deeply troubled by the condition of the scullery and of Suzy herself, just a young girl. There were stacks of dishes, buckets of water, and a large tub. Suzy's apron was wet and dirty. She was a sweaty mess too. The air in the room felt damp and hot. Laundry hung in the background. In her head, Sukey heard the haint of Aunt Sally tsk with displeasure.

They all walked down a long hallway, Miss Ann stopping to point up a stairway.

"Up these stairs is the manor house. That's where we live. You don't need to know about this stairwell. There is a maid, Truelove, who takes care of us. You belong down here."

Sukey had a feeling that Miss Ann didn't want her to know anything about the upstairs, as if she wasn't good enough. That's when the shame came rushing back.

The group walked deeper into the belly of the basement, an area with a stone floor.

"This is where the cooking is done," said Miss Ann, pointing to several cast-iron pans hanging on the hearth. "Take good care of those pans. I brought them from my home when I married Mr. Hite. You take care of them and they will take care of us."

"Yes, Missus. Us'll take fine care of 'em. You'll see."

Sukey noticed a colored woman bending over the woodpile, then putting a log on the fire. Sukey was overcome by a feeling of disgust as the woman turned toward them, her apron filthy.

"Sukey, this is Joanna," said Miss Ann. "She's been assigned here since our last cook died."

"Pleshur to meet you, Sukey."

Joanna reached out to welcome Sukey without bothering to wipe her dirty hands. Sukey wanted to turn up her nose but realized that would be impolite. Still, she struggled to visibly hide her contempt.

"Joanna is going back to the fields," said Miss Ann. "She is a much better tobacco picker than she is a cook. Isn't that right, Joanna?"

"Yes, Missus. You gots dat right."

Seeing Joanna's state of dishevelment as well as that of the cooking space, Sukey now understood why Aunt Sally didn't want just anyone in her kitchen.

"Joanna," Miss Ann smiled sharply, "you be in here today and you help Sukey in the morning with any of her questions, but then you immediately head on out to the fields. I'll be expecting the usual harvest even though you are starting later in the day. Not one ounce less."

"Yes'm, missus."

Sukey noticed a twinge of fear on Joanna's face.

Mebbe dis Miss Ann ain't dat nice afta all?

The tour continued.

"And just through this doorway is where you'll stay. We want you close to us. This family loves to eat, especially my husband. You are going to be busy."

Unlike the Shields' plantation, Sukey wouldn't have to walk far to get the food ready. Her living quarters were just in the next room. She imagined it would be nice to be near the fire during the cold winter months, maybe not so much in the height of the summer heat.

Mrs. Hite showed Sukey a pallet to the side of the room. The stone walls were cold, the room damp. Sukey noticed a small puddle in the corner, Miss Ann sensing her concern.

"The secret to curing the dampness in any room," she said, "is to never let the hearth fires go out."

"Yes Missus."

Aunt Sally's teachings crept into Sukey's mind.

"Dat is de key to life fo de slave cook," Aunt Sally had said many times. "Rain a shine, nevah let de hearth fires go out."

Following Miss Ann outside, Sukey saw Master Hite talking with an old slave.

"Sukey, I'd like you to meet Moses," said Master Hite. "Moses is going to show you around the land here."

Moses' skin appeared darker against his blue denim shirt and his pants didn't quite extend to the ground, stopping in mid-calf. Tiny strings hung from the hem. The white hair framing his mouth, along with very few teeth, suggested his advanced age. A corncob pipe hung from his lips.

"Moses is a trusted friend here. He's been here for some time and knows the grounds well." Hite slapped Moses on his shoulder. "Moses, this here is Sukey."

"Miss Sukey." Moses respectfully nodded.

Sukey noticed that Miss Ann had disappeared and Master Hite was walking toward the porch.

"Dis way, Miss Sukey," said Moses.

A few yards away, they approached a white structure.

"To de left dere is de smokehouse. We smoke most of ahr meats here. Once dey's butchahd, we hang 'em up in de smokehouse. It gets mighty hot in dere."

The smokehouse had four rooms and a cellar. One room, Moses explained was filled with brown sugar every year shoveled in with spades. In winter, they would drive up hogs from another plantation, kill them, scald off the hair, pack the meat in salt, and hang the hams and shoulders in the smokehouse. Most of the plantation's rum and wine was stored in barrels in the cellar, but there was a closet in the house where whiskey and brandy were kept for easy access.

They left the smokehouse and Moses showed Sukey the inside of the barn.

"This is where we keeps all de tools for de fahm. If you needs anything, jes talk to the ovahseah, Mastah Barton. We ain't got many overseahs here at Belle Grove. Doan need em. Revum Mastah Hite be a good man and run de fahm tight."

Outside the barn, Sukey noticed a fenced-in area that contained several different bright colors. As they neared, she saw the most beautiful vegetable garden. Plots of sweet potatoes, watermelons, strawberries, and two long rows of beehives lay before her.

Apparently, Belle Grove didn't suffer from a lack of rainfall. The vegetables were full, leafy, and ready to be picked.

"And dis gahden is for use in de house. Anything you need, you gets right here. Truelove's daughtahs, Betty an Suze, take care of de gahden."

Moses pointed to the side of the orchard.

"Dat's de burahl groun'. Down dere is where old Bob is put to rest. He was de oldest slave at Belle Grove. Dat lot fall to me now dat Bob gon."

"Well, how olds is you?" Sukey asked.

"I's 88, but massa say I only 86. Doan mattah to me. I's still lookin youngah dan ol lady Dinah and she only 80."

"Moses, I's gonna tell dis ol lady Dinah dat you say dat," Sukey kidded.

"Woan be news to her, Miss Sukey. I's out dere workin and she's on de poach sittin all day in de rockin chaih."

* * * *

Returning to the kitchen, Sukey finally got to meet Truelove, who helped straighten up her new room.

"It ain't de bes. You jist haf to make do. Jist as well, de slave quarters be full up. Plus, de Hites ran dey las cook ragged wid all dey requests. It best to keep you close here in de basemen, even if it is mongst de barrels an de boxes. An deres room foh de lil boys."

Sukey figured Truelove was in her mid-thirties but was

more interested in her formal and well-appointed maid's uniform. It was a striped, long-sleeved floor-length dress that was buttoned to the neck.

Dat dress gotta be hahd to weah.

Truelove noticed Sukey's interest in her attire.

"Sixteen buttons righ down de middle," she said with a smile. "An, Miss Sukey, if yose wondrin if dis teng is comftable, it ain't."

I like dis gal.

Truelove gave Sukey another tour around the hearth, pointing out the various utensils and where she could find sundry items in the pantry.

"Yo job is to cook de food. It be my job to suhve de food. Jest plate it up an den I's be de one to take it upstairs to de Hites."

Sukey nodded.

"De Hites gots deyselves a big room up dere," continued Truelove. "When I carry de food upstairs on a tray, I gots to put the tray on a table and serve from de side table. De food ain't nevah put on de eatin table. When dey entertainin dere guests, I carry de trays from de outside. I cain't use de inside steps. Doan make no sense, but dats de rules."

Truelove also shared the Hites' food rules with Sukey. A plain usual dinner consisted of boiled meat, greens, beans, white flour rolls, milk, and butter, and sometimes game or fish.

Suddenly, Sukey's mind went in a different direction.

Whar dem boys get to?

She ran outside to see Sam playing in the dirt with another child his age and George being held by one of the teenage girls.

I think Belle Grove is gon be all right.

* * * *

At sunup, Sukey heard rustling in the kitchen area; pots banging and clanging.

"Joanna, whatchu doin here in da kitchen makin all dis noise."

"Sorry, Miss Sukey. Missus Ann say I gots to show you round de kitchen fo I go wohkin in de fields today."

"Thank ya, Joanna, but I doan need no hep. Sukey heah now."

As Joanna removed her filthy apron and headed outside, Sukey turned her focus toward cooking, although in the back of her mind, Aunt Sally was advising.

Doan nevah forget, you in chahge of de kitchen. You owns it.

Sukey had heard from Truelove that Master Hite's favorite bread was ashcakes. Much like hoecakes, but not griddled, ashcakes were made with a meat, salt, soda, buttermilk, and a few spoons of sorghum molasses to make a stiff pone.

Sukey placed the pone on the hot hearth and let stand under the heat until a light crust formed. Then she had to cover it with ashes and cook until smoke rose from the ashes. Once the cakes were removed from the fireplace, she brushed off the ashes with a damp cloth.

As Sukey stoked the fireplace, she remembered one of Aunt Sally's many cooking tips.

"White folks food is nasty," Sally had said. "Dey doan like too much seasonin. You member dat when you cookin fo dem."

-13-

That Saturday, just after Colonel Bowman departed, Mrs. Hite came down to the hearth area.

"Sukey, tomorrow is Sunday. Here at Belle Grove, that means we all go to church. Every single one of us."

Sukey had never heard of this "church" place, but since it meant a chance to get away from the plantation, she was all for it.

"On Sundays," Miss Ann continued, "breakfast must be served early, and we'll eat before going to church."

As soon as Sukey and Truelove had a moment to relax, Sukey began the questions.

"What is dis church thing?"

"You doan know bout Jesus?"

"No."

"Chutch is wheah ya find out bout Jesus and livin forevah in de promise land."

"What is dis promise land?"

"Dat's were ya go when ya dead and live in Heaven wit Jesus."

Truelove went on to explain that Jesus was the Son of God and both of them were the Lord. She also mentioned that the slaves went to church with the masters, but the preacher would talk to the white people first.

"When Revum Mastah get round to preachin to us, he jes say be good, doan steal, doan talk back, doan run away, doan do dis, an doan do dat."

Sometimes the white folks let colored preachers preach on the lawn outside, Truelove explained, but provided them with almanacs to preach from and always had someone watching and listening to what was being said or done.

"Dey fraid de nigras gon say somethin bad bout dem," whispered Truelove. "One day we starts to sing *O fo a Thousand Tongues ta Sing* an de white folks had demselves a fit. Dey sho ain't gonna let us sing *We Shall Be Free*."

* * * *

Excited about this new adventure, Sukey got up earlier than normal.

I woke up dis mornin and musta put my body on wrong.

Sukey's joints were stiff and her muscles tight, but she had a ton of work to do. Truelove had told her that Sunday mornings were always a rush, so be sure to make the biscuits on Saturday night. Aunt Sally would have disagreed.

"Always suhve de food hot," Aunt Sally had said. "Biscuits an cohnbread need to be fresh pared so dat de butter an jam jist melt when you pile it on."

Perhaps Sukey should have listened to Truelove.

Dere is no way I's gon get dis done fo church dis mornin.

Sukey knew how to work under pressure. But that was

91

before the distraction of Truelove running around with the Master's *Sunday Best Church Clothes* that she needed to press with the iron.

"Revum Mastah needs to look his best fo preachin' de Word," she told Sukey, appearing quite nervous.

It didn't stop there. Unfortunately, Truelove found a hole in the toe of one of his socks and began desperately searching for a needle and thread. Even while she sewed, Truelove chattered that everything had to be perfect for church or Master Hite would not be kind. Sukey assumed Truelove was exaggerating.

Somehow Sukey managed to get breakfast on the table just in time. She had some honey ham from the smokehouse which she thickly sliced and slid into the middle of the fluffy biscuits with some mustard. Aunt Sally had taught her the secret to fluffy biscuits was to never twist the cup when cutting the dough.

"When you twist, it closes de edges of de dough and de biscuits caint rise good."

Master Hite was impressed with Sukey's breakfast, coming into the kitchen with a beaming smile.

"Sukey, those biscuits were just heavenly. So perfect to go to the Lord's house."

Mastah pretty excited about visitin dis Lawd person. I thought we was goin to chutch.

Sukey went back to cleaning up the kitchen when Truelove shouted from the door.

"Sukey, Master Hite already rang de 'we fixin' to leave bell' tellin us it time to load up de wagon.

There she was, covered in flour, her dress a mess.

Turned out that everyone in Reverend Hite's family

looked their best. The white women, Sukey noticed, wore white dresses with colorful wraps that tied into bows around the back of their waists.

Even the slaves looked good, nobody appearing as if they had been working in the fields. Sukey felt proud to be part of this family, even if she was dressed in a plain burlap tunic splotched with flour.

Most of the servants walked behind Master Hite's family wagon, although he whisked Sam and George up to let them ride in the back. Sukey was grateful for the assistance, particularly since it was quite a walk from Belle Grove to the Church.

Along the way, she was amazed by the size of the buildings. That said, the landscape reminded her of the market where she was first auctioned, feeling a gasp as she surveyed the town. Truelove also fretted as she watched the dust kick up, wondering if Master Hite would get his pants dirty. She need not to have worried since his feet never touched the ground until they all arrived at Saint Thomas Episcopal Church.

Master Hite helped his wife and four children down from the wagon. He even helped Sukey get the boys out of the back. As they walked into the church, the Hites were stopped and greeted by several other white folks dressed like them. With George in her left arm and Sam holding her right hand, Sukey started to follow the Hites up the steps. Moses stepped up from behind and grabbed her arm.

"No, no, no, Miss Sukey. We doan go in dere. Our place is out heah." He pointed to the patch of grass underneath the window. "We can hear all dat's goin on."

Sukey enjoyed the music.

"Dey make a lotta noise in dere," Truelove whispered, "but it ain't ahr kinda noise."

Someone sang, "A mighty fortress is our God, a bulwark never failing." Sukey had no idea what a bulwark was.

A white man dressed like Master Hite stood up and began to lecture the inside assembly.

"Our reading from the Lectionary can be found in the book of Micah, chapter six and verse eight." He paused before continuing, "And it reads, 'He has shown you, oh man, what is good and what the Lord requires of thee; but to do justly and to love mercy, and to walk humbly with your God.'"

The man talked about kindness and service to mankind being a part of service to God.

"Brothers and sisters, we have to take care of each other's needs."

I wonder if de Lawd know what dese slavers is doin? Dey ain't doin right by othahs.

It was a long and uncomfortable morning sitting on the ground, Sukey shifting from side to side on her bottom. Just when she thought the agony might be over, someone called Master Hite's name. He started talking and never seemed to stop.

"Good morning, church. Please turn in your Bibles to the book of Judges, chapter twenty, verse eighteen. And the children of Israel arose, and went up to the house of God, and asked counsel of God, and said, 'Which of us shall go up first for us to battle against the sons of Benjamin?' Then the Lord said, 'Judah shall go up first.'"

Sukey sat up and listened intently, thinking she had

heard her name. Yuda . . . it had been a long time since anyone had used her real name.

"Judah means praise," said Master Hite, who told the story of the children of Israel battling the people of Jericho. The Israelites didn't know if they could win against such a strong people as the Jerichoans. They prayed to the Lord and He told them to send the children of Judah to face them first no matter what. Judah's people were mostly musicians with horns and trumpets, not warriors or soldiers. Reverend Hite added that just as Judah held a special place in God's heart, praise holds a special place in His heart today.

"Whenever the children of Israel moved their camp in the wilderness, the tribe of Judah would go first," he preached. "Praise is powerful, necessary, and a key to God's blessings."

Master Hite concluded his talk by saying, "from a heart of thanksgiving, Judah—praise—acknowledges God's character and His mighty works. Praise declares both to God and to others His renown, fame, and glory."

Was dat why Mastah so nice to me? Was he thankin de Lawd for bringin me to Belle Grove?

Once he got done with the white folks, Reverend Hite walked outside to talk directly to the coloreds.

"Slaves, don't forget the Book of Colossians 3:22, says, 'Servants, obey in all things your masters according to the flesh; not with eyeservice, as men pleasers; but in singleness of heart, fearing God.' The Apostle Paul told the Ephesians, 'Children, obey your parents in the Lord, for this is right' in chapter six, verse eleven. Y'all are my children and my servants, so be sure to obey, and the Lord will be pleased with you. Amen?"

Those seated on the lawn repeated in unison, "Amen."

The walk back to the plantation did not seem as long. Sukey felt like she may have floated at some point. She was convinced that Master Hite was glad to have her in his family and didn't mind talking about it.

"Yuda is my real name from Africa," she told Truelove. "An now it righ dere in de Bible."

"High and mighty," Sukey heard someone mumble.

Dey jes jealous Mastuh Hite call me special.

Her happiness would not last. Back in the kitchen, Sukey heard Reverend Hite angrily yelling at Truelove.

"You didn't tell Sukey lunch is supposed to be ready when we get home from church? I just preached and I am hungry. Why ain't my food ready?"

Truelove ran down the steps in a tizzy.

"Sukey, Master real upset. He doan like bein kep waitin when it time to eat."

"I ain't know! Mastah Shields nevah took us to chutch befo. Oh me, Oh my. I ain't know! I's so sorry. I will get stahted on it righ now and I can have it ready in jes a lil while."

You done it now, Yuda!

Truelove went back upstairs carrying the message that the meal would be ready "in a little while." Sukey heard a crash of items hit the floor, later learning that Master had flipped the dishes off the table in a rage.

"A little while?" he yelled. "Tell Sukey this better not happen again!"

Sukey heard him storm out of the dining room cursing her name. Now, she could see why Truelove fretted about having the master's clothes perfect.

Truelove shouddah tol me.

Sukey began cooking, not wanting to think about what he would do if he got hungrier. She rushed down to the stream behind the barn where she kept things cool, grabbing some pickles from the bucket. She quickly sliced some tomatoes and fortunately had some biscuits left over from breakfast with a few slices of ham. She called Truelove to the hearth and told her to take the plate upstairs. Truelove looked concerned.

"Tell Mastah dis jes a startah. I'll have him some sweet taters and some chicken stew in a lil bit."

Sukey cut up some chicken and fried it in chunks until it was done. She then added potatoes, onions, and corn she had cut off the cob. After stirring in some butter and milk, she put the chicken back into the stew. As she reached for the salt and pepper, she could hear Aunt Sally scolding her for adding spices to white people's food. After adding some sweet potatoes, she sent everything upstairs with Truelove.

That should fill his belly.

Now, she had to figure out what she was going to make for supper. She sat down to catch her breath. The kitchen was a mess! Aunt Sally had taught her to clean as she cooked.

Sorry Haint Sally, I's had no choice.

* * * *

Sukey stood in the middle of the kitchen with her hands on her hips trying to think up something good to keep the master happy.

"I know," she said out loud while clasping her hands. "I's gonna make up some buttah beans an a few slices a ham wid a mess of turnip greens. An den some baked apples fo . . ."

She paused mid-pronouncement, remembering she needed a hog jowl for flavoring. Although she hadn't made hog jowls on her own before, the men had just butchered a pig. Sukey got a hog jowl from the smokehouse and washed it up.

Aunt Sally say to boil de jowl fo long time.

After it boiled, it was easy to run a knife around the pig's lip and under its tongue to get the good meat.

"Be sho to take de jawbone out befo sendin it up to de table," Aunt Sally had told her. "White folks think dey too good to eat hog jowl, but what dey know? Put dat jowl in dem beans."

-14-

T he following Saturday, Master Hite came down to the kitchen to again compliment Sukey on her meals. "Thank ya, Mastah," she smiled.

"And you will have tomorrow's meals under control, I trust?"

"Oh, yes suh."

"Excellent."

"Mastah?"

"Yes Sukey."

"I jes wanna thank ya for de preachin at chuch bout Yuda."

"Well, I'm pleased you liked that, Sukey. Judah is one of my favorite characters, amongst many, in the Bible."

"Yuda was my name when I's born, but Mastah Shields change it to Sukey."

"Hmm, that's interesting," said Master Hite. "Well, see you in the morning."

* * * *

On Sunday morning, the Hites shepherded the entire plantation once again to Saint Thomas Chapel. While the slaves sat outside, Reverend Hite mustered up the white people with his preaching. Sukey admitted within herself that she did not quite follow everything he said, but everyone around her was saying "Amen" so she assumed his message was right and good. However, during one part, the reverend looked out the window at the lot on the grass, then told the white congregation that he did not like whipping his slaves but would if they deserved it.

"Bless the rod," he said, "and him that hath appointed it. But, while I am grateful to be God's agent of chastening if I must, we ought to remember that the Book of Hebrews chapter twelve, verse six records 'For whom the Lord loveth he chasteneth, and scourgeth every son whom he receiveth.'"

To that, the white people inside offered enthusiastic "Amens" . . . outside, not as much.

After the white sermon, Reverend Hite talked to the workers about obedience and living peacefully with those who held rule.

"If we love one," Reverend Hite read from his Bible, "God dwelleth in us, and his love is perfected in us. Hereby know we that we dwell in him, and he in us, because he hath given us of his Spirit. Whosoever shall confess that Jesus is the Son of God, God dwelleth in him, and he in God."

The reverend looked up from his Bible and smiled.

"God chastens those He loves. So, if your masters whip you, is it not an act of love? You should praise God for this gift of love."

Sukey had a question but decided against raising her hand.

JOHNSON

* * * *

After the ceremony ended at the church, the human train walked back to Belle Grove. But instead of going into the house or back in the direction of the cabins, everyone kept walking past the barn toward Cedar Creek. Master Hite handed the reins over to a black worker and stood up to face the following horde, shouting as they walked.

"The Lord Jesus commanded us in the Great Commission in the twenty-eighth chapter of Matthew that we are to make new disciples and help to prepare them for eternal life by baptizing them in water and Spirit. There are some who argue that you nigras don't deserve to be baptized, but I disagree. In the eighth chapter of the Book of Acts, Phillip was riding along with an Ethiopian eunuch and talking about Jesus. The eunuch noticed the river and asked, 'Here is water, what hinders me from being baptized?'"

The wagon carrying Reverend Hite stopped short of the bank of the creek, but he kept talking.

"Now, Phillip didn't say anything about the curse of Ham against black souls, nor did he say the eunuch couldn't be baptized. He simply said, 'If you believe with all of your heart, then you can.' The eunuch replied, 'I believe that Jesus Christ is the Son of God.' Phillip stopped his chariot. The two went down into the water and Phillip baptized him."

Master Hite paused to take a deep breath.

"I don't think it's a mistake that Belle Grove sits right on Cedar Creek. I think it's a sign from God. I'm making

101

disciples out of y'all today. Sukey, let's start with you first."

Stunned by his call, Sukey was hesitant to answer and hid behind the person next to her. She shook her head and bit her lip.

"What do you mean 'no'? Here is water, Sukey. 'What . . . doth . . . hinder?'"

She could tell by his tone she should get down in that water.

Immediately, as if on cue, several slaves on the banks started singing.

> "Take me to de water;
> Take me to de water.
> Take me to de water to be baptized."

Master Hite rolled up his pantlegs above his knees and took his shoes off. The whiteness of his lower leg stood out against the darkness of his Sunday clothes. He slowly walked down into the deep creek and extended his arm to Sukey to help her down. She put a toe into the rush of water and quickly pulled back.

"Ssss . . . dat's cole!"

The onlookers started chuckling, including Master Hite. Sukey tried again, even slower. Was her reticence the water's temperature or uncertainty of this baptism thing?

"Sukey, do you believe in Jesus?"

"Yes, Mastah, suh." That was the only answer she could think of in the moment, but it seemed to make Master Hite happy.

Hite put his hand on Sukey's face, covering her nose and mouth.

"Well, then, upon confession of your faith and belief in the Lord Jesus, I now baptize you in the name of the Father, the Son, and of the Holy Spirit."

With his right hand on her face and his left hand around the small of her back, Master Hite bent her backwards and cold water rushed over her. When he stood her back up, Reverend Hite declared, "Sukey, you are now a citizen of heaven. Your soul belongs to God."

His grip tightened to a pinch on the fat on the back of her arm and he bent down to whisper in her ear.

"But everything else belongs to me."

If she had any positive feelings about this baptism ceremony, they were all wiped away in that second. She spit the water dripping away from her hair.

"There's a new name written down in glory," Reverend Hite proudly announced. "Praise the Lord! And let all who stand here today bear witness to that new name."

Reverend Hite looked up from the creek at his wife. Miss Ann scrunched her face and pointed at Sukey with her lips, like she was trying to get him to do something, like they had a secret. Isaac nodded and turned toward his young servant.

"You will no longer be known as Sukey. God has written down a new name in his Lamb's Book of Life. Henceforth, now and forevermore, we will call you Judah. Sukey has been buried in this baptism and Judah has been raised to new life!"

Praise de Lawd! I's Yuda agin!

Her hair wasn't even dry yet, but when Master Hite said his final "Amen," Yuda ran to the house.

Lawd Jesus, I gots to skedaddle. Please doan let dis

man's food be burned up!

She sped to the back of the house where the hearth was located. The smell of the beef roast she had put on the coals earlier that morning told her everything was ready. She took her pot-moving rag and pulled the cast iron dutch oven from the back corner of the fireplace. She removed the cover and heard a dry sizzle.

Caint be much juices left in dere. I's hope it's not dried out.

Looking in, she kept her silent prayers to the Lord going up. At the same time, she didn't want the potatoes, carrots, celery, and onions to be mushy. She quickly pulled the meat and vegetables out and set them on a serving plate. She arranged the vegetables around the plate. She was surprised there was still enough pan juices in the bottom to add some flour and set it back on the fire to make a gravy for Truelove to serve over the top.

While Truelove got the trays ready to take upstairs, Judah went to put together a spring lettuce salad. She realized it wouldn't stretch enough to feed the entire family. Thinking on her feet, Judah remembered Aunt Sally using dandelion greens as a filler.

"Whatchu do-in wid dem weeds, Aunt Sally?"

"Dese white folks eat de craziest mess," Aunt Sally had said. "Dese is whatchu call dandy lions. I doan know why dey call dem lions. Dey ain't like no lions I evah seen, ceptin de big yellow flowahs look like a full-grown lion's mane if you look dem straight on. Dis how you make dem. Make sho' you cut off de roots and wash de leaves clean. Let dem soak in salt and water for de mornin an afternoon. Dat take all de bittahness out. Put a ham shank to boil for a long while til it's tendah; then you throw in de *weeds*, as you say, and cook dem for a spell. When dey done, drain off de water and chop dem fine. Add some buttah, salt, and pepper. Chop up de ham in little pieces and sprinkle ovah de greens an serve dem up hot."

Judah often thought of old Aunt Sally when she cooked. *I'm so glad I put dat beef on befo church dis mornin.*

-15-

E arly morning, Judah was trying to roust Sam before she went into the kitchen.

"Owww! Mama wait," he cried.

She didn't hear Truelove come in.

"How he doin, Judah?"

"Oh, he bad I's fraid. Still sleepin way too much an still hot wit de fevah. Las three nighs he woken up drippin wit sweat."

"Sam be okay, Judah," Truelove whispered. "He a strong boy."

"I's worried, Truelove. He should be out playin and bein a lil boy, not holed up on dis pallet on de flo. Look how pale mah po boy is?"

"High yella," said Truelove. "Let's pray to de Lawd."

Judah still didn't feel a lot of trust in this God person, but she had heard Reverend Hite describe him as "a healer" and that Jesus had been whipped so his children could be saved. She wondered if Jesus was also a slave, but right now couldn't waste her time wondering about a stranger's history.

Mah boy needs help.

Judah had seen how people pray, so she bent over Sam's

pallet, clasped her hands, closed her eyes and spoke in a loud whisper.

"Lawd, have muhsee on my little boy. He sick an de Revum Mastah say youz a healer. Can you hep him? Amen."
Later that morning, Mrs. Hite came into the hearth to tell Judah what to make for supper. Judah was sitting on the steps in the doorway with her head in her hands.

"Why are you crying, Judah. Are you unwell?"

"Oh, I's sorry, Missus. I's jes so worried about Sam. He ain't gettin no better. I prayed and asked de Lawd to hep him, but he still ailin."

"Well, Master and I have a hankering for some of your chicken patties for supper and I can't have you sitting here fretting. I'll speak to my husband and maybe we can get Doc Baldwin over here."

"Thank you, Missus." Judah sat down, still worried, but less anxious.

Master Hite came down a little bit later.

"Judah, tomorrow why don't you go call on Doc Baldwin down the road and tell him I want him to come check on Sam. I can't have Sam infecting the other workers and possibly losing a strong slave. We have to get this boy well."

"Doc Baldwin, Mastah? I doan know him, suh." Her inner protector was feeling uncomfortable.

"You know him. He goes to our church and you pass by his office every Sunday. He's in the big brown building with the snake on the pole out front. You know that place, right?"

"Yessuh. Down by de town square?"

"That's right. Now, if Sam is not doing better in the

morning, I will give you a pass to get the doctor. But you need to have my lunch ready before you leave and be sure to get back in time so that my dinner is not late."

"Yes, Mastah, I sho will. I's ready stahted on dis evenin suppuh fuh y'all wid dem chicken patties an mashed taters wid gravy."

"That sounds delicious."

Seeing Master's smile made Judah's day, thankful that he would get the doctor to call on her Sam.

"Thank ya, Mastah. An how bout a nice pan a apple puddin?"

"You're most welcome, Judah. I'll leave you to get back to work. I'm already getting hungry."

In the morning, Judah sent Truelove upstairs with Master Hite's breakfast. Judah was waiting at the bottom of the stairs when Truelove finally returned, carrying the silver coffee pot.

"Mastah say he like some mo coffee."

"Mo coffee?"

Judah took the pot and hurriedly returned to the kitchen to refill the pot.

"Heah." She pushed the pot backwards into Truelove's hand without turning the handle.

"Ssss," she winced, "Dat's hot, Judah!"

Truelove shook her burned hand and cooled her fingers with her breath.

"Please take it up to Mastah!"

Moments later, Truelove came back downstairs and walked into the pantry.

"Miss Ann wants some apple jelly."

"Apple jelly? Sam, Truelove! Can you please tell Mastah

to hurry?"

"You wan me to rush de Master from de brefas table?" Truelove left with the jelly on a saucer.

Doan make me push yo up de staihs, Truelove.

Judah paced at the bottom of the steps for a sign that Master Hite was finished with breakfast. Finally, he came slowly down the stairs.

"How's our boy doing today?"

"Not much bettah, suh. Can I go call on de doctah now?"

"Yes, you may. Here's a pass that I have written for you. Just go straight down the road until you pass the Hoge's Farm. Don't stop there. You just keep going past the feed store and then you'll see the doc's office."

Quickly thanking Master Hite, Judah grabbed her satchel and was immediately slowed down at the door by Truelove.

"Keep dis pass wid you at all time, Judah. If'n anybody stop you, jist show dem dis pass and you should be fin. If'n you have any problems, jist tell dem to call on Master Hite. Now you go straight down to Doc Baldwin's and den you hustle right back heah. Doan go anywheah else."

"I'll be right back heah wit de doctah to fix up mah boy."

Judah took off in a brisk walk. Passing the silo marking Samuel Hoge's Farm, she knew she was getting close. She noticed a big colored man working in the field; he had no shirt on, and his skin glowed in the sunlight with the heat of the day. He removed his hat and bent his head in her direction.

"Ma'am."

Judah smiled but kept moving, Master's instructions crashing back into her mind.

"My name's Daniel. What's yose?"

"My name Judah."

He began to walk by her side.

"Pleased to meet you, Miss Judah. I's seen you at chuch. Judah? Didn't Revum use dat name in his preachin de otha day?" Daniel paused before speaking again. "My, I hope you doan think me disrespeckful, but you's awful purty."

Daniel's teeth reminded Judah of the ivory on the elephant's tusk and his eyes twinkled in the sunlight. She felt a slight tingle in her belly when he spoke, but she kept walking.

"I doan mean to be rude, Mistah Daniel, but my son real sick an I need to get to Doc Baldwin's."

"Oh, I's so sorry. I prays he gits bettah."

Daniel stopped, but kept talking.

"Well, I hope to see you again real soon, Miss Judah. My, that's a purty name."

She walked faster. She didn't quite like the feeling Daniel gave her. It felt like they had a past, like they had a future.

Whew, it sho is hot out heah.

Judah arrived at the big brown building and knocked, a white lady opening the door.

"What you want, gal?"

"I's sorry to bother, ma'am, but Revum Mastah Hite send me down heah to fetch Doc Baldwin to come out to Belle Grove to look at my son. He awful sick."

"*Your* son?" She seemed to choke under the words.

"Yes'm."

Judah produced the pass from her apron and the white

lady, who acted greatly bothered, read a few lines.

"Wait a minute, this says that the sick child is a Hite boy. You ain't lying to me are you, gal?"

"No, ma'am. I's tellin de truth." Judah couldn't imagine why Master had said that Sam was his son, but she was proud Master cared for him.

"I'll go get the doctor."

She walked behind a curtain and the doctor popped out a few seconds later, wiping his glasses on a handkerchief. His grey hair flopped a little as he bobbed his head.

"A sick boy, huh? Is it Walker?"

"No, suh. It's Sam."

"Sam? I don't know any Hite child named Sam. I've been the Hites' doctor for many years. I was there for each of their children's births. I have taken care of each of their children, and none of them are named Sam."

"He be my boy, suh . . . an he needs yo hep."

"I see," he paused. "Wait here." The doctor disappeared behind the curtain again, hair again bobbing as he moved.

Judah overheard the doctor and his wife talking.

"Mother, I am going out to make a call on Isaac and Ann Hite. They have a sick child out there. I am baffled why I should go out to see a sick slave child."

Judah cringed as she imagined the doctor's misgivings.

"Reverend Hite must really be desperate to ask," said the wife. "Maybe you should do it out of the kindness of your heart. The Bible tells us to take care of the preacher."

Doctor Baldwin allowed Judah to ride in the back of his wagon. She was ever grateful as she was tired after the long walk. Plus, she honestly didn't want to walk past Daniel again.

As soon as they arrived at the plantation, Doc Baldwin jumped down from the carriage and went inside to tend to Sam. Judah was relieved to see that Master Hite had moved Sam into a more comfortable spot than the floor in the back where he usually slept. Judah waited in the kitchen, wringing her hands, peeking into the room now and again.

The doctor came out with his eyes low.

"Well, you've got a pretty sick boy in there. I'm thinking it's dysentery. Has he been drinking directly from the cow lately?"

Before she answered, Judah looked up at Master Hite. He nodded.

"I doan think so, suh," she answered.

"It's a bug in his belly that just needs to pass through his system. He should be fine in a couple days."

"Thank you, Doctah fo lookin in on my boy."

Master Hite smiled as he shook Baldwin's hand. He seemed genuine in his concern.

"Isaac, since I'm here, I'll check on Ann and the new baby. She mentioned at church that she's been pretty tired since giving birth. How's she doing?"

"She's doing much better, thank the Lord. And little Hugh seems healthy and happy. She's out with the children right now, so this is not really the best time. But I appreciate you taking the time to call on us."

Judah, who had been standing off to the side, chimed into the conversation.

"Yes, thank you suh! We preeshiate it."

The doctor momentarily nodded but kept his attention with Master Hite.

"I can check back in a few days," he said. "If the boy gets any worse, give me a holler. We don't want him getting any sicker. I imagine, Isaac, you want him to grow up big and strong to be productive?"

As the doctor drove his wagon down the lane, Judah turned back toward the kitchen and met Master Hite's open hand. He slapped her hard.

"Don't you ever interrupt me when I'm talking to another white man."

Judah was stunned.

"I's sorry, Mastah!"

"You stay in your place," he snapped while returning upstairs.

Judah cried and rubbed her cheek, anger filling her mind. Still, she didn't have time to worry about how he had hurt her. Sam needed her attention and dinner could not be late.

* * * *

That evening, after most of the work was complete, Truelove asked why Judah's cheek was bruised.

"Mastah Hite hit me fo talkin outta tun."

"Oh, I's so sorry. He gets dat way. You wait, nex time he be real nice, like nothin ever happen."

"He bettah. I doan like gettin hit."

After discussing Doctor Baldwin's visit, Truelove recalled when she first started working as the upstairs maid.

"It was de summah a 1802 an I's nineteen yeahs old. Mastah was married to Miss Nelly den an she was de

113

sweetess white lady I evah seen. When I's a lil girl, her lil boy James was only three yeahs ol an he died. But den she had two mo chillen, Nelly an den James. I always wondah why she an Mastah give dere youngess chile de same name as dere fust chile dats been daid fo long time, but dey did. My oh my, Missus Nelly was so nice to me whens I stahted to workin upstaihs."

Truelove smiled, but then wiped a tear from her eye.

"Round de holidays, Missus Nelly took sick somethin horble. Mastah looka mess. He settin outside her room wid his haid in his hands. He seem to be frettin sumthin awful."

It was not the usual holiday busyness around Belle Grove, Truelove explained. No parties with friends, no merriment.

"Day befo Christmas," she sniffed, "Missy Nelly gon. Master was fit to be tied. Lil Nelly laid cross her mama feet an den she done ripped de stockins right off de fiahplace. It was de saddess Christmas. Po Miss Nelly lef dis worl so soon."

Judah had assumed that the Nelly Hite she knew—who looked to be in her late twenties—was Miss Ann's daughter. Judah had wondered why they looked so close in age.

"No," said Truelove, "Miss Ann ain't but bout eight a nine yeahs oldah dan Miss Nelly. An Missus Ann a good twenny-some yeahs youngah dan de Mastah Hite. She jes a tiny lil thing . . . an mean. I like Mastah's fust wife mush bettah. But nobody ask me a my pinion."

In the spring of 1803, Truelove had seen Master sitting in his cane chair under the big column out front. Typically, he always looked his best, but he no longer asked for his clothes to be prepared.

"He had dus all ovah his coat an it was terbly rumpled. Like he didn care no mo. An his face was old like ash."

Truelove paused, picturing in her mind his exact words.

"Oh, he love dat woman."

Truelove recalled that Master Hite was absent from Belle Grove for long periods of time after that day. He was going back and forth to a place he called Orange for much of the planting and harvesting seasons. As the one-year anniversary of Nelly's death approached, Master Hite returned from Orange with Miss Ann, his new wife.

Well, he wasn't lone long.

As Miss Ann started having babies, Master Hite had the workers add onto the size of the house, more than 100 feet.

"Judah, you shoulda see her tryin to give ordahs to the wohkas buildin on to de house? She jes a lil squeak mouse."

"Still is a squeak mouse," Judah giggled. "She look like she need feedin. I'ma have to fatten her up."

For a moment, Judah felt a wave of sorrow for Master Hite, but the fresh memory of him slapping her in the face kept her sympathies at bay.

Master Hite, Miss Nelly musta been a fine woman wut nevah sed a cross word nor treat anyone wrong. Truelove say how differnt she was compared to dis otha missus you got now.

* * * *

The next morning, as Judah soothed Sam's head with a

cool rag, she recalled Aunt Sally always swore by a secret remedy for all ailments.

Calf's foot jelly!

After silently scolding herself for not having made it when Sam was first sick, Judah went out to see the butcher for a couple calf's feet.

"What ya need dese fo, Judy," said Harry as he cut them up into small pieces.

"Gon get dat cow back fo makin lil Sam sick."

Back in the kitchen, Judah washed the feet thoroughly and boiled them in a pot of water. Once done to her liking, she drained and rinsed, then boiled them again. Wiping her brow from the puffs of steam, she eventually moved the pot onto the coals to simmer for nearly four hours. Again, the feet had to be drained, but this time she reserved the liquid, removing any fat that rose to the surface. Once the liquid cooled, it began to set. Dividing the mixture, she added allspice, cinnamon, sherry, sugar, four lemons, grated lemon skin, water and crushed egg shells to one portion. She recombined the stock with the spiced mixture and brought them back to a boil, stirring rapidly and then letting it settle while it cooled.

Boy, you bes' be glad I's ya mama. Dis is a lotta wohk!

When the jelly was done, she lifted Sam onto her lap and spooned it into his mouth. Aunt Sally had explained the medicinal and healing value, but all Judah cared about was that it worked.

Sure enough, Sam's strength returned and within a few days, he was outside running with his new friends and playing tricks on his little brother.

I loves dem boys.

* * * *

Just before Christmas, Miss Ann taught Judah how to make Brunswick Stew.

"It's a mainstay for every proper household in Virginia," she had proclaimed.

Miss Ann gave initial instructions, but Judah easily took charge, even though it was an all-day process. To make it work, Judah had to fix lunch and supper at the same time. Around noon, she would take the shank from boiling water and shred the meat from the bone. The meat then went back in the pot with a ripped-up loaf of bread, mashed potatoes, butter beans, and corn. As it cooked down, the bread would soak in all the juices and produce a tasty thick stew.

"Mastah say dis de bes stew he evah eat," Truelove told Judah after the first serving. "Miss Ann din look dat happy. I purty sho she jealous."

"She de one show me how ta make it," said Judah, baffled.

"Well, ain sposed ta be as gooda hers, I guess. You bettah hide."

Sure enough, Miss Ann marched down to the hearth next morning.

"Judah, Master Hite thought your Brunswick Stew was satisfactory, but the meat was unacceptably tough."

"I's sorry, Missus."

I swear, dis lady is one mean witch.

"And why exactly do you have the kitchen set up like this?"

Judah looked around, her jaw beginning to clench.

"Mastah Hite say dis kitchen my tertory."
Oh no, why did I say dat?
"How dare you," Miss Ann said in anger. "You may think you own the kitchen, Judah, but never forget . . . I own the food."

* * * *

After Sam's recovery, Judah's skills as nurse and medicine woman would grow, regularly being called upon by the other colored folks to fix their ailments.

Along with the calf's feet jelly, Judah used jimson weed for rheumatism, chestnut leaves and poke roots for asthma. For colds, she made a candy from horehound or just used whiskey. Consumption required a tea made from dry cow manure flavored with mint. Peach tree leaves were the main ingredient for fever or an upset stomach. Swelling or anxiety could be eased with a bath of mullein leaves. Sassafras root tea or boneset could cure a cough.

Being busy, Judah asked the workers to bring her various plants and roots from the garden, fields, or surrounding woods. That way, she could jar and store the various ingredients for every emergency.

"You is Doctah Medcine Woman," Truelove kidded.

-16-

I n the early spring of 1817, Judah began to show signs of being "big" again. Although she was unsure if the father was Master Shields or the slave broker who raped her, she found comfort that she would unlikely see either again.

Instead, Judah's thoughts regularly turned toward the handsome man she had met when fetching the doctor from town—Daniel. Her face and neck got warm whenever she thought about him.

She often had the opportunity to talk to him on the church lawn while the slaves waited on their masters to descend the church stairs.

"Miss Judah, yo boys is so hansum an well behaved. Otha chillun out heah runnin around wit no respeck fo da Lawd's house. Yo boys ain like dat."

"Dey bettah not be! Master Hite ain't de only one ta fear in dat respeck. I think I put de fear of de Lawd in em befo chuch evry week. I tell em ta sit down and shut dey moufs. Dey bettah not breathe an dey bettah not die. Dat seems to wuhk."

She smiled.

"I's jes kiddin, Daniel. Dems jes good boys . . . most de

time."

Daniel was always kind and considerate to Judah. He never commented about her growing baby belly nor even seemed to notice. Judah agonized about what she would say to explain. Daniel, she was sure, was knowledgeable about the carnal ways of white folks. Yet, she worried still.

"Miss Judah, where you learn to cook so good? I hears good things. People been talkin bout you."

"Who been talkin'? What dey been sayin?"

"Dey say you is de fines cook in dis entire valley . . . mebbe in all Virginny?"

"Who, lil ole me?" Judah playfully blushed at Daniel.

Daniel looked off to the carriages lined up near the lane.

"Dere's my missus. I should prolly go."

He turned to walk away but stopped.

"I rilly like talkin to you, Miss Judah."

"Me too." She began to lower her head in deference, but then locked her eyes on his. "See you nex' Sunday."

They talked each week through the spring and summer. Each time they met, the space between them diminished. Daniel had been born in captivity, as had his mother and father. His grandmother, he believed, might have come from the Ivory Coast.

Judah described Goga in exquisite details.

* * * *

Judah was hard at work preparing the next meal when Truelove interrupted her slicing. "Come wid me." The way Truelove tugged her arm, Judah sensed the importance but didn't appreciate being torn away from supper.

120

"Chile, I gots cookin to do," she pleaded. "You kno Mastah doan like his vittles late."

"Quit yah fussin an c'mon!"

When the duo got to the bottom of the stairs leading up to the Hites' floor, Truelove pulled Judah close to her and ducked down a bit.

"What is we do-in?" Judah wondered aloud.

"Shhh . . . listen."

Judah could hear Miss Ann and her friends in the parlor upstairs talking and overheard someone say how she got "hot and bothered" when she looked at the shirtless male slaves out in the field. Judah and Truelove sat at the bottom of the stairs and quietly giggled like children trying to keep a secret.

"Lands, Truelove, what dose women won talk bout when dey get a few glasses of currant wine in dem."

Truelove winked.

"De white folks mus nevah know you know bout dis spot."

To extend the fun, Truelove and Judah kept the food and wine flowing in a steady stream.

Mercy, dem white ladies can eat!

Judah's ears perked up when Missus Elizabeth, the mistress down at Hoge's, began to laugh and speak about her big buck named Daniel.

"Oh ladies," Elizabeth chuckled, "that man does give me the goose pimples. When he comes back all sweaty and hot, he just makes my teeth sweat. Lord-a-mercy!"

The ladies broke up with laughter, sounding like a bunch of cackling chickens.

"Truelove!" Miss Ann called from upstairs. The two

servant women jumped into action as they heard Ann's footsteps nearing their spot. They faked looking busy, Judah jumping into the kitchen to wipe the counters and Truelove dusting the doorjambs.

Stepping back to the bottom of the steps, Truelove answered, "Yes, Miss?"

"Would you tell Judah that we'd like some of those beaten biscuits and country ham we had at lunch?"

"Yes'm."

Truelove looked toward Judah, barely able to keep a straight face.

"D'jou hear dat? I guess the ladies is hungry . . . agin."

Judah hurried to the kitchen and completed her mission. She wanted to get back to listening at the staircase in case Missus Elizabeth spoke about Daniel again. She didn't know what she meant about sweating teeth, but Judah also always got a funny feeling when she thought about him too. Within a few minutes, she sent the biscuits upstairs with a bowl of jambalaya. She added some more herbs and bites of sausage that she kept hanging near the hearth after she had wrapped them in soaked corn husks.

After Truelove came back down, the snoopers resumed their place at the listening post. Sitting there reminded Judah of nighttime in Goga.

Mama an baba . . . cuddlin time.

Thinking their young child was asleep, Yuda's parents often played with each other, sometimes making noises like the animals out on the savannah. Yuda wanted to look, but never did. At times she thought her father might be causing harm, but her mother made it sound so delightful. Of course, Judah now knew what they had been doing and kind of wanted to do it too.

"And that Daniel is a wild man!" Miss Elizabeth started in again. "Now, don't tell Solomon, but that nigger, that big buck, tried to fight me off, but he knew the score. It didn't take me long to wear down his resolve."

"Elizabeth, you are incorrigible! You let a nigger bed you down? And Edward doesn't know?"

"Well, what he doesn't know won't hurt him. I just assumed he was bedding the other slave wenches anyhow. You don't think the reverend is tasting the forbidden fruit?"

"I do not," Miss Ann angrily snapped. "My husband is not a fornicating sinner like you, you shameless hussy!"

"Well la-dee-da, Missy Ann. I didn't know you were such a prude."

The party quickly turned silent. The ladies tried to maintain the friendliness, but things never again reached a level of ruckus and banter. Soon, they called for their wraps.

Judah had never been invited upstairs, but she really enjoyed ladies' nights.

Feeling a bit worn out, Judah went back to the hearth. She didn't have the energy to clean up, but she couldn't just leave it messy. Aunt Sally's haint would probably show up to scold her if she left it in even a slight mess.

As she cleaned, she thought of Daniel. Was Miss Elizabeth serious? She wouldn't steal his virtue like Crooked Teeth did to her, would she?

Judah had a momentary thought to sneak over during the night and tell Daniel about Miss Elizabeth's bragging. She even glanced toward the door. Instead, she settled herself and decided to keep her head on straight, gathering around the concept of making pork brains and eggs for breakfast.

"Lawd, I'm tired," she said out loud. "I needs ta get some sleep."

Who am I talkin to?

By sunrise, Judah felt even more worn out, having struggled through a restless night fretting about Daniel's safety. If Master Hoge found out about his wife's improprieties, he would likely blame Daniel.

She tried to ease her worry, almost relieved to get up and start fixing breakfast.

It must have been a tough night for Truelove also.

"Miss Ann act like her chambah pot doan stink. She ain't no bettah den us! She think she bettah than evahbody. She ain't bettah den anybody."

Truelove had told Judah before how sleeping on the floor outside Miss Ann's bedroom was hard on her body. Adding to that was the string tied to Truelove's leg, easy for Miss Ann to pull if she needed anything during the night.

"I knows a house slave gotta be ready to wait on de white folks, de days an de nights," Truelove agonized. "Mah life is owned by dat lady an I is nothin mo dan a slave on dat stupid string."

Hearing Truelove complain about Miss Ann was upsetting, but Judah had her own problems. How to feed the workers. It wasn't butchering time, so she really didn't have enough brains to share with anyone other than the Hites. She decided to fix up a mess of corn pone and serve it with buttermilk.

Sam ain't no fan a corn pone, but dat's what we havin today.

"I ain't eatin no corn pone," Sam protested. "I want bacon an eggs."

"Well, we ain't got no bacon and eggs, we got corn pone. And you gon be happy bout it."

He actin like dem white folk. I nevah acted like dat when I was a chile.

When Sam heard Master Hite's footsteps, he ran toward the stairs.

"I's gonna ask Papa for one a his biscuits."

"Sam, get ovah heah, boy!" Judah whisper-yelled.

"Papa, she made us cohn pone an I doan wan no cohn pone. Does I hafta eat it?"

Master Hite smiled and tapped the top of Sam's head.

"No, son, you don't have to eat it."

After a pause, he looked at Judah.

"If this boy doesn't want corn pone, don't make him eat corn pone. He can have our food. We can just give him our leftover brains and eggs . . . and George, too, if he wants some."

"But Mastah," Judah argued. "Dat ain de way it spose to be. He gots to learn to be satisfied wid whatevah he gets."

"Well, I'm telling you, Judah, that *my boy* does not have to eat corn pone if he doesn't want it!"

"Yes, Mastah." Judah burned within when Master Hite called her son "my boy."

When Master Hite returned upstairs, Sam looked at his mother like he was well pleased with himself. She looked back at him and gritted her teeth.

"When I tell you dat we's having cohn pone, you gonna

eat cohn pone. Doan you evah go off and tell Mastah bout it."

She grabbed the fat meat under his little arm.

"You understan me, boy?"

"Yes, ma'am," he whined, trying to squirm away.

"An I doan care how light yo skin is or if'n Mastah call you his boy. You is black and I is yoh mama."

Judah loosened her hold and young Sam, not quite three years old, looked his mother dead in the eye.

"Wothless niggah bitch."

Judah was stunned, her first instinct to take his head off. Instead, she ran out of the kitchen and cried.

"Where he learn dose words?" Judah would ask Truelove.

"He learn dem from Miss Ann," said Truelove. "She always callin folks wothless niggahs."

* * * *

It had only been four months since she arrived at Belle Grove, but Judah felt certain Miss Ann was showing more and more disdain.

I's sho on de missus bad side an doan know what I even do?

One evening, through the parlor floorboards, Judah overheard Ann fussing at Master Hite.

"I've seen your wanderin' eye, Isaac."

"I don't know what you're talking about."

"Oh yes you do. I've seen you staring at Judah when she bends over the hearth."

What?

"Stop it, Ann. Have you even noticed that Judah is pregnant?"

"Apparently, Isaac, you haven't noticed."

While Judah had never detected Master Hite looking inappropriately in her direction, she could tell Miss Ann was working herself up for a fight.

"I know what you slave owners do to the stock."

"How dare you, Ann. What you are suggesting is totally untrue. I am a man of the Lord."

Judah suddenly felt as if she no longer wanted to listen and walked back to the hearth, though the noise soon became louder.

That Saturday night, Judah was thinking about preparations for Sunday's vittles. Miss Ann appeared in the hearth and informed Judah they wanted roast chicken and potatoes for lunch following church. Judah wandered about the kitchen and fretted because there simply weren't enough fixings for roast chicken and potatoes. Plus, to make chicken for Sunday supper, the chickens would have to be slaughtered and plucked and blood drained on Saturday. Otherwise, the butcher would have to stay up all night and not get any sleep. Matter of fact, Judah wouldn't get any sleep either as she would have to supervise all the preparations.

Futhamo de taters from las year is all gone and it too soon fo de new taters to be dug up from de gahden.

Instead, Judah prepared beef and dumplings with some vegetables. It probably would have been a good idea for her to have informed Miss Ann of the menu change.

On Sunday morning, Miss Ann come down the stairs.

"Judah, I am not smelling any roast chicken."

127

"I know, Missus. I's had to cook beef dumplins."

Before Judah had a chance to fully explain the truth about the time constraints and lack of proper ingredients for roast chicken, Miss Ann rushed back upstairs.

A few minutes later, Reverend Hite stormed down the steps.

"Judah, you disrespect my wife, your mistress," he screamed. "How dare you!"

"But, Mastah."

"I don't want to hear it. Get out under the porch, now!"

"Please, Mastah. Please, Lawd Jesus."

Ignoring her pleas, he marched Judah outside, tied her hands together and hung them over a hook the slaves called "the swing."

"I'll be back with my bullwhip," Master Hite growled.

Her feet barely touching the ground, Judah was frantic. She had heard the rumors of servants being whipped and beaten to near death on the swing.

He knows I's wit chile. He knows . . .

Isaac returned wearing his Sunday coat, his pants pressed, his hair smoothed back, a whip in his hand. Without hesitation, he ripped the back of her dress open.

"Nooo, Mastah! Please!"

"Now, you're going to hang here. When I get back from church, you'll take your lashes and then you'll tell me how you plan to cook chicken and potatoes like your mistress told you."

She cried as he departed, everyone no doubt looking as they got lined up for the procession to church. Judah accepted the fact that nobody would take her down. And if a kind woman would come to nurse her and get caught,

Master would beat her too.

Strung up in pain and agony for hours, Judah imagined Reverend Master Hite there at church preaching and calling himself a servant of God.

When the Hites finally got back home, Judah was hanging on the swing like warm death, physical pain wracking her arms and body, her mind exhausted.

Is true dat I didn make no roasted chicken, but I doan deserve dis! Why Miss Ann hate me so?

-17-

Thankfully, Master Hite didn't beat Judah that day. Maybe he remembered she was pregnant. Or perhaps God changed his mind.

After Master ordered her release from the swing, Miss Nancy came to see about Judah. Nancy wiped Judah's forehead with a wet rag as she laid on her pallet.

"Dem preachahs is jes as bad an mean as anybody else," Nancy whispered. "My formah mastah was a preachah. Folks called him a good preachah, but he was one of the meanest mens I ever seed. He done so many bad things till God kilt him."

Nancy, who was about 40 years old, turned the rag on Judah's forehead.

"Stay clear of Miss Ann till her anger cool off," she advised. "She come down the steps, make your way out to de gahden. She come out dere, go into de smokehouse. She ain't neva gon come ovah dere."

Nancy started to make some okra stew to comfort Judah.

"I doan make it good as you. Talk me through it."

Following Judah's instruction, Nancy diced onions, deseeded a hot pepper, crushed garlic and ginger, and put it together in a paste with a bit of pepper. She fried the onions in oil and added the garlic and ginger mixture. After those flavors came together, she mixed in some chopped tomatoes and oxtail stock. Taking off the tops and bottoms of the okra fingers, she finely diced the remains and added them to the pot of soup. She let everything cook down on the low part of the coals until it turned into a thick stew.

They talked all the while Nancy stood and stirred over the pot.

"I member dis one time," said Nancy. "On dat ol plantation I truly did hate, de front steps was real high an one day dis slave gal fell down de steps wid her baby chile. De revums wife and daughter hollered and went on terrible . . . and dat poor chile was hurt so bad she coulda been dyin. When de marster come home dey was still hollerin. When dey told him bout it, he picked up a board and hit de poor chile cross de head and kilt her right there. Then he told his slaves to take her and throw her in de river. Her ma was screamin too, but he made dem throw de chile in. It made no sense fo dat man to kill his own slave. He jis mean is all."

"Lawd, dey jes throw dat po baby in de river?" Judah tried to sit up.

"Chile, doan get up. You need to rest. Lawd know, Mastah Hite ain't near as mean as dat otha preacha, but he ain't gon let you be off from work much longah, so you betta take whateva rest you can get."

Judah knew Nancy was right. There was little time for play or rest at Belle Grove. Even the small children were assigned tasks. They hunted eggs, gathered pokeberries, shucked corn, and drove the cows home in the evening. Little girls knit stockings. There wouldn't be much patience for a cook to rest.

When Judah did go back to work, she kept Miss Nancy's advice in mind. She tried her best to stay out from Miss Ann's way, but Judah could still sense the anger.

Eventually, however, everything slipped back to normal at Belle Grove—whatever normal was.

* * * *

"Judah, there's a big holiday coming up next week and I'm gonna need for you to plan a feast for about 50 people from the church," Miss Ann pranced down the stairs, smoothing her skirts as she walked. "It's Independence Day and we want to have a grand spectacle . . . food, family, a full spread."

Later, Judah found time to question Truelove.

"Evrah summah de white folks get all cited and go to celebratin. What so speshul bout dis fof of Joo-lie?"

Truelove chuckled.

"Oh, dats de day white folks celebrate bein free. Revum Hite splain from de pulpit how he fought in de Big Wah to get de Independence from England. July fourth is sposed to be de day when all mericans be free an all men created equal. Uhh, equal? What I think dey mean to say is all white men is free and equal."

"An what do dis mean fo us colored folk?" asked Judah.

"Well, uh, it's a celebrashun day fuh you too." Truelove smirked. "Once you fix all de food fuh de guests, you kin have the rest of de night off to watch Mastah's firewuhks light up de sky."

On the morning of July 4, 1817, Judah rose way before daylight. The evening before, she had enlisted help for a pig roast. She asked Anthony and several of the men to get involved with the slaughter of the pig, setting up the pit, preparing all the firewood, and taking shifts all night to keep the fire going and turn the meat on the spit. Judah took the time to have the pig cleaned up for the roasting. It had made horrible noises when the men stabbed it with their knives and it took five strong men to lift it high enough to let the blood drain out. Anthony had skinned the giant beast slowly, being careful to cut all the fur off. When the skin was pulled all the way off, Anthony opened its belly up and out poured the innards.

Reverend Hite came out of the house to complain about the smell.

"Doan worry Mastah," Judah assured. "Once dem pig guts is cleaned an boiled, de stink goes away."

As he hurried back into the house, Judah remembered the first time a pig had been slaughtered in front of her.

"Ew, dat's horrble!" she had said to Aunt Sally.

"Hush up, gal," Sally had laughed. "All dat will be on your plate soon enuf."

When the pig for the Hite's party was fully dressed, Judah sewed up its belly while leaving a small hole to stuff with cubed bread, butter, pepper, salt, sage, and thyme. After Judah completely sewed the hole closed, she put the pig's liver, lungs and feet on the fire to boil. Once the liver was cooked through and soft, she rubbed it between her hands until it was fine. Then she chopped up the lungs and the meat from the feet to make mince. The innards went into a skillet with the pot liquor and thickened with butter, flour, salt, pepper, and sage. Anthony had saved the pig's head which, once cooked, Judah laid on a dish with the mince. It was an all-night cooking affair that lasted well into the holiday.

"Dat's a lot of pig." Judah said to Truelove.

"Missy spectin a heap a folk."

Sure, it was a lot of work, Judah thought, but when the Hites entertained, the slaves would also get some extra food. And a whole pig!

We gonna cook up errthin from de roota to de toota.

Judah envisioned the tasty chitterlings. Master and his family didn't like them, so when they finished butchering the hog, Judah got the odds and ends.

Mmm, dems good eats! Mastah doan even know dat he eat dem all de time. What he think he bin eatin fo breakfuss? Scarfin down all dem sawsidges. Dems filled wit de chitlins of de pohk meat afta I clean out de innards.

* * * *

Marcus was born in August of 1817, Judah somewhere in her early twenties. It was still hard to imagine herself as a mother to three boys. As a child, she had envisioned someday marrying Dinka and raising a family. Judah loved her children . . . they just deserved better.

* * * *

In the fall, it was time to prepare Belle Grove for the holidays, family arriving from many directions. James

Madison, the fourth president of the United States and the brother of Isaac's first wife, Nelly, visited during Thanksgiving.

At the listening post on the first day of President Madison's visit, Judah overheard Master Hite talking with his former brother-in-law.

"So, Mr. President, how are things over at Montpelier?"

"Everything is just fine, Isaac. Life is so different now that I'm finally out of Washington. Eight years. I think Dolley misses it more than I do."

"How is Dolley?"

"Oh, fretting her fiftieth birthday next May. Hah, I hit that milestone fifteen years ago."

"I'm 59 now," laughed Master Hite. "I'd love to be that young again."

"See, I guess this is why we both have young wives."

They both laughed, Judah unamused at their good fortune.

"I do miss your sister, James," said Master Hite, the conversation turning somber.

"What's it been, fifteen years? I miss her too, Isaac."

"Nelly was my most amiable wife, the dearest object of my affection," said Master Hite in a slow, somber voice. "She submitted to her fate with a resignation and fortitude indicative of an innocent and virtuous mind. We were married and deeply in love for twenty supremely happy years. I can truly say she always appeared to be as dear to me as my own soul. I prayed for her to be healed, but the Lord took her to be with Him."

"Amen," said Madison.

There was a lengthy pause. Perhaps both were drinking

some of the Master Hite's favorite whiskey.

"What's happening in the tobacco business?" asked Master Hite.

"Not much for me, I'm afraid," said Madison. "I went into the White House a much richer man than I am today. Not only has the price of tobacco been plummeting, but I can only tell you the farm was badly mismanaged while I was away. Got a lot of work to do, but I do love Orange County, so we'll figure it out."

Another pause.

"But, Isaac, your place seems to be thriving."

"More than 7,000 acres of grain and livestock with a sawmill, distillery, gristmill, and general store."

"How have your crops fared?" asked Madison.

"We have been extremely seasonable, sometimes with an excess of rain falling in torrents. One summer it considerably injured our wheat. But the prospects of corn I never knew more promising."

"Well, Isaac, you've certainly been successful enough to maintain a strong population of slaves."

"Over 150 at this time, Mr. President, but it all started with the gift from your father back in 1783. When Nelly and I married, my father deeded us 483 acres and yours afforded us fifteen slaves. Of course, most of them are dead and buried, but their sons and daughters serve us still. Your father's good faith in me as a young man and gift of trust paved the way for all that I now have. I am also grateful the Lord taught me how to be a good steward of those gifts."

"If this whiskey is any indication," said James, "God also blessed you with one of the finest distilleries in the south."

Both men laughed, Judah imagining them slouching in their chairs.

"What's your thoughts on the slave situation, Mr. President?"

Judah's ears perked up.

"Still struggling, I suppose. You know, we both were raised on plantations and thereby realize the importance of the institution of slavery to the economy of the entire South."

"I agree," said Master Hite. "I couldn't operate Belle Grove without slaves."

"But at the same time, Isaac, I deeply worry about the instability of a society that does depend upon slavery."

"But I would argue, Mr. President, that the people up north do not have the right to tell us down south what we can and cannot do."

"I think my concern goes even beyond that, Isaac. Let's just imagine that, next month, Congress votes to abolish all slavery. What, I ask, will happen to all the slaves? How could the coloreds possibly integrate within our society?"

Who dese guys think dey foolin.

"I totally supported the notion back in 1808 to ban the international slave trade," Madison continued, "because that was simply barbaric. That said, I also do not like Washington interfering with our homegrown slave population."

I ain't homegrown. I's glad to head back to Goga.

The conversation went on late into the night, Judah losing interest that either of them had the power or inclination to improve her destiny.

Over the days Mr. Madison was on the Belle Grove grounds, Master Hite demanded that everything be special. He particularly wanted his guest to be well fed, so Judah cooked up a storm.

While the former president complimented every meal, he really loved Judah's special shortcake.

"De men upstairs gobbled it all up," Truelove told Judah. "How'd you make dat?"

"I jes bakes up some conebread real thin-like an cut it into squares. On one layer, I puts a slice of ham then covers that with another piece of conebread. Den I adds some chicken breast sliced up fine. Conebread again an lightly browns up some mushrooms in buttah an add some flour and milk to make some nice gravy ovah de top."

* * * *

As Christmas approached, Reverend Hite had been pulling double duty at the church.

"Christmas is the birth of our Lord," he said. "Every detail has to be perfect."

The reverend even took Judah's jars of fruits and vegetables she had stored and said he was going to give them to "the poor and needy amongst us."

Seem to me, you caint get mo poh an needy than de nigras on dis here plantation.

It was nice to see Christmas return. The happiness and slower pace seemed to lift the white people's spirits, who seemed significantly thankful to the Good Lord for the harvest and the bounty that was now in the pantry.

Jesus' birthday was also a nice time for the servants.

Nobody got whipped during Christmastime. It felt to Judah as if everybody—black and white—had joy and hope for the new year.

She also noticed the holidays increased white folks' appetites. There would be from four to six kinds of meat pies in stacks, cakes of every kind, plenty of sauces and jellies, preserves, relishes, and pickles.

Dem folks can stuff it down!

And, it was Judah's responsibility to keep them fed.

She was getting Christmas dinner ready when she had to spank Sam's hand for stealing out of the salad she had mixed up. That brought tears.

"It's bettah for you to cry now," Judah scolded, "den for me to cry later cause Mastah Hite done strung you up for stealin outta his plate. I know he say you kin eat his food but let him give it to you . . . you doan jes take it."

Master Hite must have been feeling the warmth of the season—or perhaps the whiskey that was flowing like rain. He pulled all the house servants together and presented everyone with gifts of extra clothes and instructed Judah to prepare extra vittles. Judah took his kind manners as the right time to ask him about Daniel.

"Mastah, I's been meanin to ask you. Can I get a pass to go down to Hoge Farm?"

"Down to Hoge's . . . whatever for?"

Judah blushed. With her head down, she whispered, "To see Daniel."

"And who is Daniel? Are you sweet on him?"

"Yessuh." Judah swished uncomfortably, keeping her head down in embarrassment and fear.

"De las time I seed him at chuch he say he wants to

marry me."

Master Hite looked at Judah with surprise in his eyes.

"Judah, slaves marrying off the plantation doesn't make much business sense. I do agree that you are of marrying age. Maybe it is time for you to start thinking about a husband. What do you think about Milly's boy, Anthony?"

"A-A-Anthony, Mastah?"

For the next few days, Judah couldn't get Daniel out of her head, the thought of him making her quiver deep down.

She approached Master Hite as he sat out on the porch steps smoking a cigar.

"I begs yo pahdon, Mastah Hite. I doan means to botha you reposein."

Judah bowed herself near Hite's feet, aiming to speak to him about her marriage to Daniel, but the reverend quickly dashed her hopes.

"Judah, Anthony will make a perfect husband for you . . . and will give me, I mean, us, some strong children. I'm thinking after the spring thaw we can get you two hitched."

"But Mastah, ifn I's to get married, I wish you'd considah me marryin Daniel down to de Hoge's."

Judah couldn't believe she was being so forward, but constant pining for Daniel made her brave, she guessed.

"Daniel, huh? Like I told you before, that might make a tricky situation between two plantations. I'll talk to Mr. Hoge about the arrangement though."

Master Hite sat back with his pipe, the smoke curling up as he sucked and exhaled.

Several days later, after a meal of chicken and dumplings, Master Hite pulled Judah to the side.

"Judah, as I suspected, marrying Daniel is going to cause more trouble than it's worth. It's unnecessary and just doesn't make good sense. You should marry someone here on Belle Grove."

Master Hite paused.

"Yes, the best solution will be for you to marry Anthony. He's about the same age as you . . . good looking and strong."

"Anthony, Mastah? But, Daniel."

"You may not be happy about the arrangement, but Anthony is one of our own."

Judah realized Master Hite's mind was set and no amount of protestation would bring satisfaction. And most likely it would get her punished.

Later in the evening, after she finished her chores, she met Truelove under the big tree out back.

"Ole man Hite say I gots to marry Anthony. I ain't intrested in dat boy. He all quiet an all. Plus, he dote on his mama too much. Whatchu think?"

"I doan know. I thought he a hansum boy. You caint see it coz yo min stuck on Daniel. An dere ain't nothin wrong wit dat boy takin good keer of his mama."

"Truelove, I likes Milly, but dat ain't no reason to marry her boy."

"Listen Judah, a boy who take keer of his mama, fo sho take keer o' his wife."

"Mebbe yous right, Truelove. Yous a good fren."

Judah's spirit quieted as they continued to talk under a full moon. Judah leaned back against the tree.

"You know, Anthony is a good boy. He fetched watah for me befo an brought me fiyawood last week to stoke de fiyaplace."

Within the week, Master Hite called the plantation together for the big announcement.

"We're gonna have us a slave wedding here at Belle Grove. Judah is going to marry Anthony."

No one was more surprised than Anthony.

* * * *

Later that evening, Anthony visited the kitchen, awkward and nervous. Which was exactly the way Judah felt.

"Miss Judah, nobody tole me dat you and me was gonna get married. Did you know?"

"Sorta. Mastah Hite tole me I's to get a husbun an you was his bes choice."

Anthony looked confused.

"I thought youse sweet on dat guy Daniel dat I always seed you talkin to at chuch."

"Sorta. But Mastah Hite say he caint marry no puhson who doan live at Belle Grove. An dat's why he say I gotta marry you."

"Hmm," said Anthony, trying not to look hurt.

"I's sorry, Anthony, it ain't I doan like you. I jes doan know you is all. Mebbe we's gonna be purrfek for each otha. We jes gots to know each otha bettah and I guess we's gonna bein married an all. I's willin to gives it a try."

"Yes, Miss Judah. I's willin too." Anthony grinned. "Specially since we gots to anyway."

Judah gave Anthony a hug. It was not how she pictured falling in love.

* * * *

"After the last of the winter snow, Master Hite told Judah to start preparing herself to be a wife.

"The deed will be done when the weather breaks," he said. "You are going live with Anthony in that cabin over yonder. I'll give Anthony some time off to fix it up."

The night before the wedding, Judah had fallen asleep on her pallet and didn't hear Master Hite come into her room.

"Judah, wake up." She opened her eyes a crack to see the lantern in Master's left hand.

"Mastah, every thang all right? You hungry? Want me to fix you sumthin ta eat?"

"No, you come with me." He walked out of the room taking the light with him. Judah fumbled around in the dark until she found her bearings and followed Master Hite outside. Moonlight and the lantern helped her notice that he had a bullwhip flung across his shoulder.

"Where we goin Mastah?"

"You just follow me."

"Yessah."

Behind her master, the two entered the cabin where Anthony and his father slept. They must have heard the approach because the lantern lit upon two scared faces. Master Hite called out in a low whisper as if he was sorry to wake them.

"Anthony, come here, boy."

Anthony stood up off the floor and appeared before Master Hite.

"Pull off your shirt," said Master Hite.

Everyone, including Anthony, looked confused. Anthony, though, did what he was told without question. Judah watched Anthony's chest muscles as the lantern's light flicked. Master Hite smiled a little watching her watch Anthony.

"Now, pull your pants down," Hite added.

Anthony's eyes widened and he turned to look at his father and back to Judah as if he was looking for help or permission. He got neither.

Hesitantly, Anthony untied the knot of the rope around his waist and his pants fell to the ground about his ankles.

Master Hite turned to Judah with a big grin on his face.

"Judah, do you think you can stand this big buck?"

Judah's face heated up as she looked upon Anthony's glory. She lowered her head and giggled from embarrassment. She had never looked upon a man like that . . . naked.

Master Hite put his hand under her chin and lifted. She looked at Anthony up and down.

"Yessir, I guess so," she said, again trying to hide her face from looking at Anthony's naked body, but also wondering about Master Hite's intentions. Again, her face was lifted by the reverend. She swallowed, a big gulp of spit filled her mouth.

Are my teeth sweating?

Master Hite thanked everyone and left the cabin. Judah, after one final glance at her future husband, followed with trepidation.

I ain't ready fo dis.

* * * *

144

The morning of the wedding ceremony, the grannies helped Judah get dressed. The seamstress had fashioned a linen dress with a white sash.

Judah loved the dress but protested when they began to press her hair with the hot iron comb to make it straight. It was bad enough the comb burned her scalp, but she had wanted to wrap her hair in the African tradition she remembered.

"Oh, Miss Judah, you is such a beautiful bride. You an Anthony will have such strong chillen."

Reverend Hite conducted the ceremony on the front porch of his home. When Judah stood before Anthony in the presence of Master Hite, who looked so official wearing his black church suit, she bowed her head and closed her eyes. Looking back up, her open eyes alit on Anthony's smile.

His teeth are so white. I nevah noticed how his eyes spahkled befo. My Lawd, he is hansom.

The reverend read from the Bible about the wife submitting to her husband. Judah also heard something about obeying Anthony because he was the "man of the house." After a few more instructions, Reverend Hite declared them husband and wife "by the power vested as the owner, master, and keeper of said slaves."

After the ceremony, Judah and Anthony were surrounded by friends when Master Hite interrupted.

"Anthony and Judah, y'all are married now. The Bible says in Hebrews 13:4 that marriage is honorable in all, and the bed undefiled; but whoremongers and adulterers God will judge.'" He paused. "Well, it's time to get down to business."

Master Hite expected the couple to "make marriage" in his presence, and they did not have the option to not perform.

It was awkward, but Judah did the best she could to shut out Master Hite's presence. Apparently, Anthony did the same.

After consummation, Judah acknowledged to Anthony she would forever honor their wedding vows. In her mind, Judah knew Anthony was kind and figured she would learn to love him. She also assumed she would never have another man forced on her.

After the wedding night, Master let Judah and Anthony be alone for a couple of days, but he did come back every so often to see how the couple was getting along. Master Hite told Judah the more children a slave had, the more they were worth.

"And you are worth a heap," he said. "Your three boys are as strong and healthy as mules."

Except for the time Sam had dysentery, they were never sick. Having the medicine woman cook as a mother probably helped.

Anthony and Judah's cabin was located out near the old peach tree in the orchard. With ripe fruit from May through October, Judah told Anthony she would jar up peaches to make cobbler when he came in from the fields on Saturday night.

Anthony was an exceptional builder, handyman, and field worker; but had almost no understanding of cooking. When he asked how she was going to create a cobbler, she was more than happy to tell him.

"I put de peaches in de cast iron skillet an add a little

nip of sugarloaf and cinnamon. I stir it all aroun wit a little bit of flour to thicken up the juices. You followin me, Anthony?"

He smiled, enjoying the excitement in his young wife's voice.

"An then I mix up some dumplings from flour, salt, butter, a little sugar and milk to make dough dat I can spoon in lumps on top of de peaches. I jes cook em over de coals for a spell and you, my husband, are gonna have peach cobbler."

"I can almost smell it, Judah. You de best cook evah."

* * * *

When Uncle Edmond, the negro preacher, came through the area, Judah asked him to also perform a marriage ceremony. After praying for the couple before a gathering of their friends, Uncle Edmond said, "Come on, Anthony, you and Judah gots to jump ovah de broom. You do that so to see which one is going to be de boss of your househol."

He was serious. Uncle Edmond held the broom about a foot high off the floor.

"The one that jump ovah it backwahds an nevah touch de handle is gonna be boss of de house, an if both of you jump over witout touchin it, there won be no boss; you both jes be frenly an cheahfahl."

Anthony got all tangled up in that broom and fell headlong.

"I guess I's in charge," Judah giggled.

-18-

"Judah, you is so beautiful. And you is all mine."
Judah rolled over into her husband's arms. She had been sleeping when he lumbered into the cabin after sundown.

"It has been a long week and us is so glad to see you," he whispered into her ear.

Judah smiled, giddy with warmth. It was good to have Anthony home, even if it was just for a few hours. A worker of significant skill, Anthony had been hired out by Master Hite to work on another plantation. Anthony had learned the trade from his father. He could build about anything, even make spinning wheels and parts for looms. Sometimes Hite let him have wood to make furniture out of leftover lumber for his own household. He was a very valuable man.

Judah seldom had Anthony all to herself.

Dem otha mastahs work him so hard . . . from cain't see to cain't see. Dey calls it "gettin dere money worth."

Anthony's entrance had roused Judah from her slumber. By the time she became fully aware of his presence, he had already pulled off his shirt and was starting to take his pants down. Master Hite was nowhere in sight, so

Judah took some time to really look at him. She remembered Master asking if she could "handle this big nigra" and she told him she could. Last week, Judah admitted to herself that relations with Anthony did, in fact, hurt a little bit, but she wasn't sure if her discomfort was Anthony or the fact that Master Hite was standing there making sure his investment was going to work out.

In Anthony's arms, she wasn't somebody's cook or somebody's mama, she was this man's wife. He watched her undress, looking at her as if inspecting a ripe pepper on the vine. He took the time to study her, tracing her frame with his eyes. Was she ripe enough for him?

Judah stepped out of her dress and he interrupted, "Judah, what happened to your legs?" He was looking at the scars across both legs, caused by an accident that occurred when she first worked for Aunt Sally. Pulling a pot off the fire, she had gotten too close to the coals and the hem of her dress caught on fire. Aunt Sally immediately poured a bucket of water on her to put the fire out and followed with a lesson.

"Chile, doan you know you have to hike up your skirt tails when you get close to de fireplace? Dat, or call on me to hole your dress up to void such a happenin. I spect you to do de same fo me. We is a team in de kitchen. We gots to look out fo each other."

Judah never liked to show her scars and tried to hide them, but Anthony pulled at her dress.

"Oh, no ma'am. I ain't mean for you to covah up. I ain't meant no harm and I dint want to shame you none. You's beautiful, Miss Judah."

He kissed her lips and kissed down her entire body. He

held her legs and gently kissed her scars. She felt loved and was impressed with his level of nurture . . . much like he did when their boys scraped their knees while playing. But this didn't feel like a daddy kissing his boys; it was a grown man kissing his woman.

"And I's all yours, Mistah Anthony."

At that, he lifted Judah off her feet and cradled her in his arms. Judah felt so safe with him, like he wouldn't let anybody get at her ever.

He laid her down on the mattress Judah had stuffed with fresh wheat straw. She wasn't worried about whether the bed was strong enough to hold them. Anthony didn't seem worried about it either.

Soon, Judah was making the same sounds she remembered her mother had made on nights with Baba. It all made sense now. She felt a few drips of water fall from her eyes. She quickly tried to sniff them back into her head. Anthony heard her sniffle and stopped his hammering.

"What wrong, Judah? What you cryin fo?"

"You gon think I's crazy. I was jes thinkin bout my mama. Bein wid you make me think of home. I miss my mama."

Something within her broke and a flood welled up in her face. This time, she didn't try to hold it back. She just let the tears come. She thought about Mama, about Baba, about Goga.

"I just doan wanna be here no mo, Anthony. I wanna go home." She gasped for air as she cried. Her crying mimicked that of her boys crying deep sobs when they would get a whipping.

"You is home, Judah. Everwhere I am wid you is home

to me."

Judah glared at him.

"Belle Grove ain't none of my home! I am a child of Goga! I doan belong heah."

The more Judah cried, the more Anthony squeezed. It felt like she was in the coils of a boa constrictor.

"Anthony, I cain't breathe."

"Oh, I's sorry."

He loosened his grip, but he had made his point. She was his. He was going to take care of her. She didn't have to worry. He was her man—*mlinzi wangu*.

She felt safe again. Later, she must have whispered aloud "my protector" because he stopped smoothing her hair and said, "What dat now?"

Smiling, Judah drifted off to sleep in his arms.

In the morning, Judah got up a little earlier than usual. She had slept so well, felt so rested and energized.

She wanted to make breakfast for Anthony before she made it for anybody else. She didn't have much in the cabin since they hadn't received the monthly allotment. So, she used ground parched corn for coffee and cane molasses for sweetening. Turned out, they had enough to drink and even provide for the neighbors.

She assumed Master Hite was up and expecting his breakfast so he could get down to the church house. Running to the kitchen, Judah made him some johnny cakes by mixing up some cornmeal and white flour with baking soda and salt. She poured in a cup of cane syrup and some lard. She mixed that up and baked them in a pan. The pan had a top that was covered with hot embers from the fire to ensure the browning of the bread on top. That way, the bread would bake up evenly and wouldn't be gummy when she took it out. She also fried some eggs.

"You jes in time," said Truelove.

"Is a miracle," laughed Judah. "Get dat man fit fer preachin.'"

Judah didn't want to risk not having Master's Sunday lunch ready, so she put a roast on to simmer. There were racks fitted in the fireplace to hang pots. She had the big pot setting on the fire. As the water boiled, the meat turned over and over, swimming to the top and going down again. Judah wanted to make sure the meat would be tender when they got back from church, so she set it down in the coals and rushed off to trail the Hites behind their wagon.

Anthony dawdled behind, waiting for Judah before he began the trek. He walked alongside his wife, holding her hand as they went to the church house. She felt like a young girl walking along the river bank back home. Anytime she looked up, her eyes met Anthony's. He smiled; she smiled back. It was a new experience being with him on the church lawn. Her feelings felt weird. It was not like she had never seen him before, but somehow now he was not a stranger, not just someone enslaved on the same plantation. Now, he was hers. Through the window, the white folks had struck up singing "What a Friend We Have in Jesus." Judah wasn't thinking about Jesus today; all she could think about was *her* Anthony.

The service concluded and as they walked back to Belle Grove, the dread of Anthony's upcoming departure was already starting to overwhelm her. It was a feeling she would come to expect every Sunday evening—the time for her to prepare for the long week at Belle Grove with Anthony somewhere else on loan.

Sam had really taken to Anthony.

"I love you, Daddy," he cried out, "an I doan wanna see you loaned out to no othuh place. You needs to stay heah."

"Yeah, big man, I love you too. But dis week I gets to go to workin at young Mastah Hite's Guilford House up in White Post. I be back Satday evenin, soon as I kin."

Anthony kissed Judah and began the long walk down the lane on his way to young Master Hite's. Each departure made Judah's heart hurt. Anthony took a piece of her with him. She didn't know how she was going to make it through the week.

"Judah!"

Ann Hite's call broke her from her spell. She wanted Judah to prepare for a guest for dinner. Truelove was already upstairs in the manor house getting the table ready. She had polished every piece of silver in the house.

Missus didn't specify who the special guest was, but Judah decided to go all out on the dinner by roasting a small pig. First, she rubbed pomegranate juice all over the meat and made a dressing of stale bread and hickory nuts. She sprinkled the pig with salt, pepper, and flour.

"Well, lil fella, into de clay oven you go."

Judah looked forward to the kitchen filling with the smell of roasting pig. She had dotted the flesh with pats of butter to help with browning because Master Hite loved the cooked skin, especially if it crackled when he bit into it. When the pig was roasted, she placed it on a big platter, an apple in his mouth and circled with molds of hog's foot jelly. He was ready for the table.

The special guest was Miss Ann's brother, Jonathan Clark.

Judah was glad she'd made a big meal. Truelove started the feast by serving a dried pea soup Judah made by boiling dried lima beans with onions, pepper, and salt for a couple hours before passing everything through a sieve. Judah put the beans back in the liquor with a healthy pat of butter and some flour and slices of salt pork for seasoning. She pounded a spoonful of celery seed to add to the mix and served it with some toasted bread that had been diced and fried in butter. She put the croutons in the tureen before adding the soup.

To round out the meal, Judah included some collard greens for good measure and a ginger cake for dessert.
As Mr. Clark left that evening, he noted his sister's hospitality.

"Ann, thank you for your cooking. You laid out quite a spread and I feasted sumptuously."

"Certainly, Jonathan. It was my pleasure."

Judah sat at the listening post, seething at Miss Ann's acceptance of the compliment.

-19-

"Ann, look at this! Look at this!"

"What is it, Isaac? What's going on?"

"Look at this headline. 'Dr. Robert Berkeley Murdered by Slaves, Body Stuffed in the Fireplace.'"

Judah could hear the noise.

"Mercy, in the fireplace," she continued to half-talk, half-shriek. "And set him on fire. His slaves lured him into the cabin where they told him they were holding a runaway slave. When he came in, two others jumped him and beat him to death."

"Where did it happen?" Master Hite asked, his voice mixed with concern and anger.

"Sweet Jesus!" Ann gasped in horror. "Rock Hill in Frederick County. That's not even thirty miles from here, Isaac. They better hang those murderin' black bastards. I don't trust any of them."

"It's a horrible happening, Ann, but let's remember to be Christian about this. Not all nigras are bad."

"Why are you always defending those savages?"

"I'm not defending. Just trying to do what the Good Book says . . . no judging, right? We don't even know all the facts."

"The fact is, Isaac, this proves that you can't trust them. What's stopping them from doing that to us? You even let them have guns!"

"For varmint killing!"

"And white folk killing," Ann snarled.

"That hasn't happened, Ann."

"Yet!"

"Do you know how much we've saved on rations for the slaves since they've been allowed guns for hunting?"

"You're the one who decided to feed them so high on the hog. They're animals, Isaac . . . livestock. They should eat what the other animals eat. I think you forget, sometimes, they're slaves, not people."

"What are you talking about, Ann?"

"I mean exactly what I am saying. You let them walk all over you."

"We don't have to treat them horribly. Maybe that's why they turned on this Dr. Berkeley. Our nigras are fed, satisfied, and well taken care of. We get plenty of work out of them, so I don't see what the problem is."

"The problem is, husband, I don't want to get killed. If we treat them like people, they will forget their place. You've got them out there with the finest things. What do slaves need with a lamp chimney? All that says to me is that we don't work them hard enough. They should be aching to go to sleep when they get done working for the day, not setting up with a night light. They're probably meeting in secret and plotting against us."

"You're being hysterical. We've had no insurrections. Our slaves have never given us any reason not to trust them."

"Yeah? What about Primus? Has he ever been found? Who's to say he's not planning to come back here and murder us in our sleep. Think of the children, Isaac."

"No, Primus has not been found yet, but one thing I'm sure of is that he's not hanging around waiting to kill us."

Judah heard a chair being moved.

"I'm getting one of my headaches," said Master Hite. "I think I will retire for the night."

The next morning, the argument began again. Truelove had just walked down the stairs and signaled Judah to come listen.

"Ann, you look a fright. You're sitting in the same spot I left you in last night. Are you unwell?"

"That's what you're asking me? Am I unwell? You walk in the room and find your wife in the same seat you left her in hours ago and that's what you ask? Am I unwell? No, I am not well! I'm scared, Isaac."

Judah and Truelove heard Master Hite walking toward his wife.

"What are you afraid of, dear?"

"Don't dear me," she said. "I read the rest of that article. You need to hear what those slaves did to poor Dr. Berkeley. They planned out that killing. The leader, Randolph, disappeared from Rock Hill for several weeks. How long did you say Primus been gone?"

"A few weeks."

"My exact point. This Randolph was pretending that he had lost the use of one of his hands to keep from working. One of the *trusted* female slaves, Sarah, told Dr. Berkeley to come to the cabin because Randolph had returned. Berkeley was smart enough to take his pistol with him. He didn't get a chance to use it because Randolph tripped him and grabbed a club and beat him repeatedly. Poor man cried out for help, first to Sarah then to Ralph. Neither one of them helped. They beat him until he was dead. And then they threw his body in the fireplace and burned him to a pile of ashes and bones. Pick your jaw up off the floor, Isaac! You see, we can't trust these brutes."

"Does the article say anything about how Dr. Berkeley treated his slaves? For them to do him like they did, I imagine he wasn't too kind. Plus, I will tell you again that our slaves are good people."

"That's what you take from this story? Good? That's the problem. They ain't good. They ain't people, Isaac."

The two eavesdroppers heard the wrinkle of the paper opening and being slammed on the table.

"Listen to this, Isaac. Court testimony stated that the conspirators burned Berkeley's body because they decided it was the best way to conceal the evidence of the crime. Evil, Isaac, evil. Apparently, in court, the woman slave, Sarah, was so pleased with their actions that she screamed, 'The devil is dead and we burned him!'"

"See," said Isaac. "She called him the devil. He had to be cruel."

"Are you not listening to me? They searched his pockets and took his keys. They kindled a fire with coals and the article says they were wicked pleased to bring wood to Sarah so she could feed the flames. The next morning, the killers went back to work as if nothing had happened. And you, Isaac Hite, think we should trust them!"

"Look, Ann, nothing I say right now is going to satisfy you or stop your fear, but I stand by our slaves. They are a part of our family."

"Our family?" Ann growled. "They are not family. We own them, Isaac. If you think they won't kill us, you're of unsound mind. I wouldn't put it past any one of them. What's worse is the article says Randolph is still on the loose. He's probably somewhere teaching Primus to come back here to do the same thing."

"Don't be so hysterical, Ann," Isaac said.

* * * *

Judah made fried chicken and potato salad for supper that night with pickled cabbage. She had quartered a head of cabbage, sprinkled it well with salt and let it remain for three days. After that, she washed off the salt and put the cabbage in a preserving kettle with weak vinegar and simmered over the fire for half an hour, then drained it dry and placed it in a jar and poured boiling vinegar— spiced with onion—over it.

Judah had gone back to work fixing dinner for the slaves when she heard Truelove running down the steps screaming, "Miss Judah! Miss Judah!"

"What wron, girl?"

"Miss Ann on de warpath sayin you tried to kill de Master and her."

"What you sayin? Slow down an tell me what's goin on. She say I tried to kill Mastah?"

"Yeah, Mastah was chompin down on his chicken like he ain't nevah et befo an den he took a bite of dat pickled cabbage an he went to coffin an hackin sumthin awful. Miss Ann stan up an say, 'See, I tol you Judah is tryin to

159

kill us! You believe me now?' Mastah jes kep chokin an spittin. She poundin his back de who while."

"I ain't tryin to kill nobody. If'n I wanted dem daid, dey'd be daid a lon time go."

Fortunately, there was no further word from the Hites about being murdered by the cook. Nevertheless, the sting stayed with Judah for quite a while.

-20-

As she stirred, Judah's mind drifted to Anthony. She really had learned to love him. Judah especially loved Saturday nights. The week was certainly long, but it all seemed to wash away when Anthony stepped foot into their cabin. It wasn't long before Judah found herself big again.

On one Sunday morning, Anthony scolded his pregnant wife for carrying firewood for a large pot of water she needed to boil. Anthony said it was his job to do those types of tasks.

Judah returned, "Anthony deah, I done toted many an armful of good ol hickory bark to cook with. When I gots work to do, I ain't got time to be waitin on you to move things for me. What I'm gon do if you ain't here?"

* * * *

As fate would have it, both Judah and Miss Ann were pregnant for the fourth time. At this moment, they were each eight months pregnant and in their nesting phase.

Chopping vegetables, Judah eyed the chair and wished she could take a break to rest her swollen ankles. She also noticed Marcus toddling her way.

"Marcus, baby, I caint play righ now. Let Mama be. I gots to keep makin Mastah's suppah."

Judah bent down to turn her young son away from the chopping table.

"Heah, play with Hugh."

The Hites' son regularly spent time in the kitchen. At three, Hugh was a year older than Marcus, but they were equal in size. Judah picked both boys up and put them in the corner with some whole potatoes to roll around. She smiled at them and patted the two boys on their heads.

Dey so sweet. Dey's good boys.

Judah went back to fixing the food. It wasn't long before the boys were getting in the way.

"Lawd, dese two."

Judah returned her focus to stripping string beans, suddenly realizing the boys' giggles had quieted. She noticed Marcus still playing with the potatoes, but Hugh was gone. She glanced around the kitchen to see Hugh playing near the red hot coals and fire.

"Hugh, get away frum deah!"

Judah snatched him by the arm and pulled him to safety. As any scared mother might react, she smacked Hugh's bottom.

"You know bettah," she scolded. "What I tell you bout gettin by dat fiyah?"

Hugh screamed like Judah was killing him.

"Hush up dat caterwaulin, boy! You gon' distuhb yo mama an daddy."

Wut I say dey fo? He gon really scream now.

That he did.

"What's going on down there?" Miss Ann yelled from the top of the stairs.

Judah grabbed the rag off the table and began wiping her hands to tidy up.

"Nuttin, Missus. Hugh an Marcus down here makin a ruckus."

"Mama!" Hugh waddled up the stairs crying louder as he went. "Judy hit me!"

"She what?"

Miss Ann stomped her way down the steps, not stopping until she stood near Judah in the winter kitchen.

"Did you hit my son?"

"She did," Hugh pleaded. "She hitted me right on my bottom."

Miss Ann spun around and looked Judah straight in the face. With every word, she took a step toward Judah and reiterated.

"Did you put your filthy black hands on my son?"

She didn't seem to care about my black skin when I was feedin him and she was sleepin.

"Yes'm."

Judah prepared to explain how Hugh had almost been burned up by the fire, but before she could get the words out, Miss Ann slapped her across the face.

"Don't you ever put your slave hands on my son again. He's gonna be your owner and master someday."

"I's sorry, missus."

Once again Judah's words were preempted by Miss Ann's right hand.

"Who do you think you are, you black cretin? You need to know your place!"

Ann turned her back and stormed away. Halfway up the stairs, she turned around and came back to where Judah and the boys stood. She grabbed Hugh by the hand, wrenched him up on her hip, and then carried him up the steps.

Judah settled Marcus, who was now crying, and returned to work.

The whole time Judah beat on the dough, she couldn't help but wonder what Miss Ann would do if her son had fallen into the fire.

Bettah fuh me to cry now den you to cry later, Miss Ann.

-21-

George tumbled into the hearth room, tripping over the threshold of the doorway and nearly stumbling over a basket of corn cobs.

"Mama, is it time for Sam and me to eat? We hungry."

"Yes, baby. Gonna fix it up real soon. You go get ya brutha."

Judah wanted to give them some of the chicken stew that was left in the soup pot, but she did not dare serve them the master's fixings. Instead, she stirred up corn mash with some of the liquor from the sweet potatoes. She knew it would take some time to get the dish ready, but that would be no problem. She guessed it would take a while for Sam and George to both come back. They usually had to wrestle and chase each other around first. She also figured they would come back dirty, and she was right.

"Where have y'all been? De food is ready."

"I went all ovah and found Sam down at the stream tryin to catch tadpoles in his hands."

"Well, George, youse wettah dan Sam," said Judah.

"Sam got me wet, Mama! When I tole him you wanted him fo dinnah, he grab me and push me in de watah."

"No, I didn't, Mama," the older brother pleaded. "I

slipped on de side and accidentally landed on him and he fell in. It was a turribal accident."

"Well, ya'll go in dere an wash your hands in that cool-in watah bucket. And den come back an eat. I gots to get dinner stahted for mastah."

* * * *

Judah's fourth child, Milly, came along just before dawn on the second day of June 1819. Hers was a rough birth. To Judah, it seemed like Milly was fighting just to survive. *Lawd, give dis baby strainth.*

As she had done when Marcus was born, Nancy served as midwife. Nancy prided herself on her midwife technique and never failed to mention she had eleven of her own. When Truelove wasn't being called upstairs, she helped by following Nancy's orders, as did Anthony's mother, Milly. To complete the generational cycle, Aunt Jane hobbled in to watch. Grannies proclaimed it their duty to catch the baby.

"I is here," said Aunt Jane, probably the oldest woman on the plantation. "Les gets dis baby into de wurl."

Despite her pain, Judah managed a smile toward Aunt Jane, for some reason remembering her age.

"Mastah tell me dat I is eighta-seven," she once told Judah. "But dat caint be. I is eighta-nine if I a day."

Miss Ann, who herself was due at any time, said Judah could have just a few days to lay up and rest after the baby was born. When the white women of the plantation had babies, they were treated kindly by doctors and midwives who let the new mothers stay in until they were fully recovered. The enslaved midwives and the old grannies wanted to be strict on womenfolk after their days of birthing. With the missus' permission, the grannies took care to do the new mother's work for a short spell. The idea was to let the mother set up on the fifth day, walk outdoors for a short stroll around the house, and get back in bed. That didn't always fly with the masters.

When Anthony returned home on Saturday evening, three days after Milly was born, Judah thought he was looking a bit poorly. He said his rations had run out a few days before. All he'd had was some cornbread and water. Someone of his size and strength needed more than cornbread to stay healthy. Sadly, Judah didn't have much to give him, since she hadn't been back to work in the kitchen.

The boys were asleep and Judah had just finished feeding the baby.

I caint let my man go hungra.

She had Anthony lay down and pulled him close to her chest, feeding him like she fed Milly. Anthony complained, but didn't stop sucking once the sweet milk touched his lips. Judah's heart warmed as she looked down at the dependency in Anthony's face as he fed. Her nipples hurt as Anthony drew his large swallows, but she was glad to do it. Now, he really would know how much she loved him.

Seeing Anthony suck at her breast gave Judah new energy.

I think my layin up time is doane.

The next morning, a Sunday, she dressed and wrapped the white apron around her waist. Judah felt the pride of a Gogan boy who had passed the manhood trials and had been handed his first hunting spear. It was time to go back to work.

She walked back into the kitchen to find the scullery maid—Abba's 17-year-old daughter Winna—fretting over a bowl of something. Winna's anxiety was punctuated by the flour that covered most of her dress, arms, face, and hair. And Miss Ann was standing right behind her.

"Missus, what you doin in de kitchen?" asked Judah.

"Oh, Judah, it's about time you got yourself back," Miss Ann angrily snapped. "This wench has no idea what it takes to run a kitchen. We haven't eaten good for days and, with my baby coming any time now, I need good food. I was just giving her the instructions on getting lunch prepared before heading off to church. Get this gal and this kitchen in order."

"Yes'm. You get yosef dusted off and get upstaihs and fix yosef up. Judah's got this. You need to get yosef ready. You be one of de finest ladies at de church house, fo sho."

Miss Ann wiped her hands on her apron and cast it away as if it were covered in the plague.

Goodness, de missus is big. I's hope she doan go havin dis baby righ heah on de kitchen floh.

"Judah, I'm so glad you're back," Miss Ann spoke in a more polite tone as she began a difficult climb up the steps.

Winna grabbed Judah's arm.

"I's even mo glad youse back, Judah. But Milly only three days ol and youse workin already. Youse need to be restin."

"Winna, wit you help, we can do dis."

Miss Ann allowed Judah to stay back from church that

day. To add some nourishment to the meal, Judah decided to make potato pone. With Winna's help, they grated raw potatoes into a bowl with an egg, sweet milk, butter, and a double grating of nutmeg before adding a handful of flour and two heaping spoons of cane molasses. The mixture went into a skillet with a flat top and Judah covered the pan with red hot coals. The potatoes baked until tender.

Tater pone and cold sweet milk make a mighty fine supper.

* * * *

On June 9, 1819, one week after Milly arrived, Ann Hite gave birth to a daughter. Miss Ann had been in the kitchen area barking orders when she suddenly crumpled on the ground.

"Judah, come help me stand up," Miss Ann cried.

"Winna's righ outside de doah, Missus."

Judah yelled for her helper, then quickly turned back to Miss Ann.

"I's sorry I caint, Missus Ann. De grannies say I ain't loud to lift nothin heavy while I'm healin."

"You will do as you're told, Judah! You listen to your mistress, not some old slave women. I need your help."

Judah hesitated, balancing her health against Miss Ann's wrath. Fortunately, Winna ran into the room.

"Winna, hep Missus Ann get up and den go get Nancy to hep her.

"Yes'm, Miss Judah."

As Winna charged out the door, Judah momentarily

169

left Miss Ann's side to call upstairs for Truelove to bring Master Hite. A minute later, when Winna returned with Nancy, Ann was a ball of sweat, crying out in agony between heavy breaths.

"Judah," said Nancy, "you gots a pilla or somethin soft to lay behin Miss Ann's haid?"

"All I gots is a bag a flour we jes got in wid de supplies."

"Dat'll haf to do. Bring it heah."

Judah ran to the corner and grabbed the flour sack. As she prepared to foist the large bag, she paused to remember how she had just told Miss Ann the grannies' prohibition against heavy lifting.

"Winna, carry dis ovah to whar Nancy an Miss Ann at."

"Yes, ma'am."

Winna carried and positioned the heavy weight behind Miss Ann for her to rest upon. Once Miss Ann was in the appointed position, Nancy commenced to raising Miss Ann's dress so she could get a look. Miss Ann tightened her legs and angrily pushed her dress down.

"No, Nancy. What are you doing? You can't look at me there."

She tried to continue her lecture on impropriety but was interrupted by a stroke of massive pain.

"Missus, I doane birfed haf de chillun at Belle Grove. You doan hafta worry none. I's seen plenty a lady pahts. Seent one, seent em all."

"You have birthed half the slaves at Belle Grove," Miss Ann managed to yell, "but I forbid you to touch my lady parts."

Ann screamed again.

Nancy again tried to reach under Ann's dress.

"I said doan't touch me. Get a real doctor."

"Missus, dis baby comin an I need ta get ya drawers down so I kin see."

As Ann pushed the fabric of her dress deeper betwixt her knees, Nancy turned to Judah.

"Judah, we need some hot water."

"Already gots it ready."

Winna placed a bucket of hot water just out of Miss Ann's reach. As Ann kicked and screamed, Aunt Jane arrived.

"I hear's deres a baby to kitch," she beamed.

"You jes in time," commented Judah.

Master Hite was also just in time, followed by Truelove rushing down the stairs.

"Isaac, Isaac," Ann screamed, still clutching the cloth of her underwear while fighting off Nancy's hands. "We need Doctor Baldwin."

Nancy pulled away from Miss Ann's dress and looked squarely in Master Hite's eyes.

"Massa, by de time Doc Baldwin get heah, dis baby be doane come. I's right heah. I kin birf de baby. It be best for my han to be in de right place fo kitchin dis baby."

"She's right, dear," said Isaac, talking quickly in the panic of the moment. "Just let Nancy finish the job. She's qualified."

Miss Ann pushed herself upright on the sack underneath her, her nostrils flaring in anger.

"Isaac Hite. I am not giving birth on a stone floor with some nigger hands up my dress! You get me upstairs to my bed and you call on the doctor and get him over here to help deliver your child like a proper lady."

Despite his advanced years, Mr. Hite quickly lifted his wife into his arms and carried her up the stairs, Truelove allowed to follow.

"Well, dat's bad," said Nancy. "Dat coulda be my fuhst white baby I brings into de wurl."

"An I sho wanted to kitch one of dem white babies," Aunt Jane added.

"Les hope de good Lawd let dat baby wait for de doctah," whispered Judah.

The downstairs ladies watched as Master Hite mounted his horse and raced toward town.

Nancy returned to the field, Aunt Jane went back to her rocking chair, and Judah went back to cooking with Winna. In a matter of time, Master Hite and Doc Baldwin returned.

Later, Truelove would tell Judah that Doctor Baldwin had hardly put down his satchel when Miss Ann pushed out the baby girl.

"Lucky dat baby didn't drop on de flooh," Truelove said. "Doc Baldwin tell Mastah he shoulda call soona cause de protracted labah doane tuckered out pooh Miss Ann an he coulda relieved somma de pain and sufferin."

They named the baby Matilda.

* * * *

In the fall of that year, Aunt Jane took sick. Nancy's ten-year-old daughter, Evelina, ran for Judah to hurry down to Jane's cabin. When Judah saw Jane laying there, she felt death all around.

"Medicine woman," Jane mumbled.

"Aunt Jane, I's gonna fix you up better dan new," Judah lied.

Worn from nearly ninety years of struggle, Aunt Jane winced with every cough. To make matters worse, her body had swelled and she complained her chest hurt.

Although Jane had no children at Belle Grove, she had plenty of friends, each wanting to help. Judah instructed Hannah and Eliza to set her in a warm bath made of mullein leaves. During the evening, Emmanuel searched the creek bank for some boneset. The tea Judah brewed tasted bitter, but Jane was able to sip the crushed leaves and flowers down with brown sugar.

When that didn't ease the bad cough, Judah put a plaster made of mustard seeds and flour on Jane's chest.

Judah also took some parsley from the herb garden and asafetida to hang around Jane's neck. She believed asafetida's horrible stink would ward off any more sickness and the death spirit until she could figure out something stronger. Judah called it the "devil's dung."

Judah tried everything she knew, but Jane's strength and fight diminished with each cough, each breath.

Despite her ministrations, Judah could not find a cure.

"It fine, Judy," whispered Jane between coughs. "I gonna see my mama and papa and even some my chillen, I spect. Heaven be near."

Aunt Jane died the next morning, Judah at her bedside.

Death had big plans for Auntie an he doan let go til he claim her for his own.

Aunt Jane was buried that evening. Truelove and Judah washed her up and put a pretty dress on her body. Both ladies cried quietly as the menfolk lowered Jane's body into the ground. Once they covered her up with dirt, Judah put a hole in Aunt Jane's cook pot using a hammer and nail.

"Why you doin dat, Mama?" Sam asked.

"Dis way de spirit rest and doan wander."

Suddenly, standing by Jane's resting spot, Emmanuel burst out a low soulful tone from deep within his belly.

> "Good-bye sistah, good-bye sistah,
> If I doan see you moah;
> Now God bless you, now, Jane,
> God bless you, If I doan see you moah.
> So good-bye, sistah, good-bye, sistah;
> Now God bless you, now God bless you."

The gathering sang along with Emmanuel, tears in every eye. Heartbroken, Judah looked to the sky.

Live forever, sweet Jane.

* * * *

The next day, Judah was back at the fire, her mind on Aunt Jane.

Mighty sad fo sho. Times like dese call fo comfit food. Speaks ta de soul of man, quiets im down.

"I've got peace like a river in my soul," Judah quietly sang as she rolled dough.

She doane wit dis here cruel world. No mo' feelin de lash, no mo chains, no mo Mastah. She gone to Freedom Land. She gone home wit de Creator.

Judah felt a little bit jealous of Jane. She wasn't as much

scared of death as hopeful where her soul might travel.

I wanna go back to Goga. I wanna see my mama. I hope she daid. I hope she aint langishin in slavery like me. I hope she jump off de boat befo dem people got to dis here hell.

-22-

For some reason, Judah's mind had drifted to the market. She had to be no older than 13. Women screaming as their children were being ripped from their arms. Husbands tearing at chains trying to reach their women, now bent over and fingered for public inspection and display.

She blinked, demanding her mind to stop, to once again attempt to somehow block the horror.

-23-

As she rolled out biscuits for the night's supper, Judah thought about their life. Although she only got to see Anthony less than two days a week, somehow the kids kept coming. Milly had been the first girl in the family and Mary followed in 1821.

When little Anthony was born in 1823, Judah surveyed her young family. Sam was nine years old, George seven, Marcus almost six, Milly four, and Mary two.

Six chillen. Sho is busy roun heah.

* * * *

Sam caught a rabbit and brought it to the cabin late one Saturday evening. Earlier that day, he had set the trap in a bush where he knew rabbits came at night. Judah had mocked him when he'd set up the little wooden box.

"Rabbits is fast," she told him. "You gon need to be fastah to kitch him."

Sam looked up at his mother and smiled.

"I's gon get im, Mama, jes you wait an see."

Ain't no way he gon kitch that thing.

"When you kitch it, I'll make us a big pot a rabbit stew.

177

Dat sound good?"

"Yes, ma'am. Wid taters an carrots?"

"Fo sho. Caint think of makin it any otha way."

"Can you make it wid de good gravy an biscuits to sop it up wid?"

"Sho can, but fuhst we gots to kitch dat rabbit."

At that, Sam ran out the door to hunt for wild game.

The fire outside the cabin had burnt down to kindling when Sam came running out of the bush later holding a live bunny by its two ears.

"See, Mama? I got im jes like I sed."

"Well, looky-here. I gots me a lil hunta. Bring im on ovah an let me get a look at de po lil fella."

The rabbit wriggled and bucked trying to escape from Sam's hands.

"Hol him tight now," said Judah. "Doan let im get away."

"I got im tight, Mama. He ain't goin nowhar. An even if he do get away, I'll jes kitch him agin."

Judah bent the rabbit's head backwards and Sam squealed, "Mama, doan hurt im!"

"How else we gon have dat rabbit stew you asked fo if'n we doan kill de rabbit?"

Judah grabbed the rabbit from Sam's hands and broke its neck with lightning fast speed.

"Ooh, you did dat so fast. Doan dat botha you?"

"No, baby, I's been doin that a long time. Rabbits, possums, coons, tree rats . . . all of em is good eatin."

Both Sam and George were in the habit of being helpful around the cabin, playing hard, and constantly competing against each other.

While Sam was now the hunter, George liked to fish. A

few days after Sam captured the rabbit, George brought in two small fish he'd caught down in Cedar Creek.

"I broughts dese home fo dinnah," he said proudly.

"George, dey's too small fo de ho famly. We'd need Jesus to do a miracle fo real like Revum Mastah was talkin bout."

"But we eat Sam's stupid rabbit."

"But dese jes pitiful lil fish. You go kitch something biggah."

George stormed out of the cabin, mumbling under his breath and dragging the two small fish on the pole through the grass. A few days later, he came running into the manor house kitchen with a couple of big fish.

"Look, Mama, look!"

"Oh, I can sho use dose. Lay dem right here on dis table."

Judah had not decided what she'd make for the Hites that day, so George's catch was great. That said, she really didn't like to cook fish. It took a lot of time and effort to pick out all the bones. It could easily be ruined if cooked too long or too fast. Plus, it wasn't an easy process to cook fish on an open fire.

Once the fish was filleted, it had to be gently pan-fried. Once fried, it needed to be picked apart into pieces. There was also the mixture of flour, milk, onion, butter, and salt that had to be stirred atop the dying coals until thick. It was hard work.

George was excited that his mother would serve his fish to Master Hite but disappointed that he would not get to taste it.

* * * *

179

Taking a momentary break from preparing the fresh fish dinner, Judah noticed Master Hite out on the porch playing with Sam, George, and Marcus. The game of tickle tag had the boys screaming with laughter.

What bothered Judah the most about Master Hite's attention was the effect it had always had on Sam. George and Marcus not so much, but Sam really took to heart being called Master Hite's son. More and more, Sam began to assert his *specialness* . . . to own his white identity.

Every so often, Judah had to slap him down.

* * * *

Anticipating the reaction upstairs to the fish dinner, Judah settled into her usual snooping place at the bottom of the stairs. She took great pleasure in people enjoying her food. This night, however, Master Hite was up in arms about something he'd read in the newspaper.

"They doane let some uppity nigra graduate from Middlebury College in Vermont! Some nigra named Alexander Lucius Twilight! What is wrong with these northern do-gooders? What's next?"

Judah imagined Master Hite's face changing colors as he spoke. He really couldn't hide it when he was angry. She didn't need to imagine Miss Ann's anger; she could hear it.

"A nigger college graduate? Whoever heard of such a thing? How'd he do that? Niggers can't even read."

Miss Ann's irritation seemed a little exaggerated to

Judah.

Betcha I could learnt to read if'n I woulden get whipped fo havin a book.

Judah had heard of college, Master Hite sometimes recalling his days at William and Mary. She figured college had something to do with reading but wasn't quite sure.

Mus be impohtent if de white folk gettin so agitated bout negroes goin dere.

Judah wondered if she would live to see the day when any of her children would graduate from college, whatever that might be.

* * * *

Several days later, Judah was near the garden scolding Sam for teasing George when Master Hite approached from the house.

"Judah, you need to teach your little nigras that they need to learn to stay in their place," he grumbled sternly. "Not Sam, not George, not Marcus are going to get any special treatment like they give nigras up north. Part white or not, these boys are nigra slaves and they ain't getting no education."

Master turned and walked away.

Sam was devastated.

Judah's first inclination was fury, her second to calm her son.

"Mastuh din mean dat," she said, kneeling and trying to hug him. "I knows he din mean dat."

Too late. His eyes swollen red with tears, Sam pulled

from her grasp and ran like a wayward wind across the field.

Judah worried, then wondered what Anthony would have done. Of course, he had been loaned out for the week, hoping to return on Saturday night. But even then, she should dare not tell him. He might do something awful. They'd put him on the swing.

She did tell Truelove the full story. They found a few minutes together as Judah prepared the fixings for supper. Seemed like the two best friends were always sharing their secrets and pains.

"Now I gots to go back up dere an face dose white folks," Truelove growled after hearing of Master Hite's insult and Sam's heartbreak. "Lawd, keep murdah outta my mind."

The chicken was frying when Truelove returned to the kitchen, happily sniffing at the aroma.

"Judah, when you fry dat chicken, the angels sing from heaven."

"Well, dat mighty nice of you to say," Judah smiled.

"I saw you out dere tryin to catch em," said Truelove. "All that cluckin an fightin all ovah de place. Dem chickens hard to catch."

"But aftah you wring dere necks, they ain't so hard no mo," Judah laughed.

"You gotta secret for cookin em up so good, Judah?"

"I jes gets the bird plucked up and den dusts it wit some garlic an pepper an salt. An den I drag it through some flour an put it in de hot oil. Makes de hearth smell so good."

"Master Hite sho do love it," said Truelove. "Hopeflee it'll take de mean outta him."

Truelove winked and whispered in Judah's ear.

"An save some fuh me. You know, de part you doan poison."

* * * *

Finally, it was November 6, 1823. Judah had been looking forward to this day for weeks. She had spent much of the afternoon making two cakes, one for the Hites and one for the party.

That night, she closed the kitchen much sooner than usual, then briskly walked, cake in hand, to Truelove's cabin.

"Dis is so excitin," said Truelove's mother, Sarah. "She ain gon see dis comin."

Judah placed the cake on the table and was immediately hugged by Truelove's two daughters. Betty, who worked as a seamstress, was 28, and Suze almost 17.

Judah felt Suze's baby girl wrap tightly around her leg.

"Eliza, yose sho is purty," said Judah as she leaned over to pick up the toddler. "Wish I had me a granchile."

"Try havin a great granchile," laughed Sarah, who was now sitting in the rocking chair. "Caint believe mah lil guhl, Truelove, tuhn fohty yeahs ol today. Wisht I's fohty gin. Dis fifta-sevun wearin me down."

"Granny," Suze said. "Yose ain ol . . . yose jes ain young."

The laughter and kidding had barely subsided when the door squeaked open.

"Happy Buthday," everyone chimed.

Truelove was shocked.

"Lawd, I doan know whatta say."

"Dat a fust," laughed Sarah.

"An Judah, I knows yose uppa somethin all day," Truelove nearly shouted as she eyed the cake. "Do da Mastah and Missus Ann knows you doan did stolen dere cake."

"No, an dey ain gonna know," laughed Judah. "We gon eat de evidence righ now."

And so they did, a wonderful birthday party. Truelove even got to blow out a candle.

* * * *

Next morning in the kitchen, Truelove was still giggling.

"Judah, wisht I know wen yo buthday wuz. I get yo back fo sho."

"Mastah say it was some day in 1794. An I bin figurin I mus be bout twenny nihn . . . or mebbe a hunerd an nihn."

-24-

Nearly three weeks had passed since Judah had seen Anthony and she'd been deeply anxious. A hard worker, Anthony was also talented. If something needed built, repaired, or lifted, Anthony was prized.

Master Hite had loaned Anthony to his oldest son, Isaac, who had been deeded a farm about a half-day north of Belle Grove in Winchester. Isaac Hite was 18 years old and needed help.

Even knowing where he was working gave little comfort to Judah.

The kids also worried about their father. Two-year-old Anthony had repeatedly asked when Daddy was coming home.

"He gonna give me a hohsee ride."

"Doan worry, Lil Anthony, Daddy ain't forget."

Anthony was no doubt missing all seven children, the latest—Maria—born February 15, 1825. Now three months old, she was sweet and always slept the entire night.

Judah worried. The last time she had seen Anthony, he was close to burning up with hatred toward his overseer at young Isaac's farm. Judah prayed Anthony hadn't lost his temper or done anything that would get him in trouble.

Since Saturday was her one day off in May, Judah spent the day mending the children's clothes. She also cooked a small meal with a raccoon one of Truelove's boys caught. Judah just might have been the best coon cooker in Virginia. She would take a fat raccoon and dress it clean. Judah would rub the meat with fine-ground red pepper, dust it with salt, put a little water in the pot and cook it about two hours.

"Take dat ol coon off de fire an sprinkle some vinegah an a dash a sugah," she told Truelove. "Oh, an plenty flour, buttah, an black peppah."

As it browned, she'd pour hot water on to make brown gravy. Judah preferred cooking in the cabin rather than in the manor house even though she had to make up some of the ingredients and skip a few cooking steps.

Wished I had some conemeal dumplins righ now. Jes gotta make do.

It was twilight and Judah started to think she wouldn't see Anthony for yet another week. She lit the evening candle and, turning around, saw Anthony's big frame filling the doorway.

"Anthony! Whar you bin?"

"Oh, Judah, it's so good to see you."

He reached out for Judah's embrace and she excitedly wrapped her arms around his broad shoulders. She heard him wince a little bit, but he didn't make a big deal about it so neither did she. She squeezed him for what seemed a lifetime. She melted like candle wax in his arms. All was right in her world again.

"Anthony, why it's been so long? You alright?" While

she talked, she began taking her clothes off, longing to feel his naked body up against hers. She pulled his pants down first. She wanted him to know what she wanted.

Anthony pulled back from Judah.

He nevah done dat befoh.

"Judah, give me a chance to get in de house. I need to see de chillen."

"Dey's already sleepin. I wasn't sho you was comin."

Anthony lifted the candle and walked quietly over to where the kids slept, kissing each of them on the forehead.

"You'll see dem good in de mornin."

Just before Anthony blew out the candle, he began to slowly remove his shirt. He had his back to Judah. She waited with anticipation, loving the way he made her feel.

"Anthony, what happen to yo back? Whar dem scars come from?"

He tried quickly to turn his back away from her, but it was too late. Judah had seen the marks.

"You got a whippin?"

"Two weeks ago. Master Hite went crazy on me! He had gave me a pass to go into town to pick up supplies. Somehow, somewhere, I lost de pass. Dis white man stop me and axed to see my pass. He say 'Where is you goin, boy?' I tole him dat Master Hite sent me to de stoh. I couldn't find my pass to show im, so he called fo de sharif. I guess de sharif believed me cause he took me back to de house. After he left, Master looked at me wid fire-like in his eyes an cused me of tryin to run away."

"Wuz you?"

"Judah, do you think I's gonna leave without you and de boys? What kinda man you think I is?"

"I wouldn't be mad. I be real sad, but I'd be happy to know you found freedom from dis way of life."

"Even tho I have to live way from you summa de time. Even tho I only get to see you two days de week, I will nevah leave you. I's yose fo life."

That's all he needed to say. Judah flung her arms open wide. Oh, how she had longed to feel this feeling. She tried not to grab him too hard around the back, but every now and then could see his pained face in the moonlight. She amazed at how this man knew how to make her feel so good! He touched her in all the right places and in all the right ways.

Come morning time, when she could see better, Judah inspected the sores on his back.

"Anthony, you sed dis happen two who weeks ago? You sho bout dat? Some dese sores is still open an pussin. Who de nurse over dere? She ain't doin no good job!"

"Ain't no nurse."

"Dat jes ain't right. Somebody spose to tend to de sick an ailin. Doan worry. Judah will fix it up right."

She took out her tin of wound salve she had cooked up the last time there had been a whipping on the plantation. She'd made it of beeswax, crushed comfrey, and lard to help it smooth better.

"Imma smooth this on an send some back wit you. You need to rub this in mornin an agin at night. Is dere some-one over dere dat can rub dis on you?"

"Yes, Miss Judah. I think dere's someone who can do it. Prolly not as good as you do, though."

He playfully nudged his wife with his right shoulder.

Until that moment, Judah didn't have a reason to hate

young Master Hite. She had practically raised him, and he knew the *right* way to treat the slave folks. Still, he had beaten Anthony, without cause. Now, her nicety toward the young master turned sour.

I hate de Hites! In fact, I hates all white people. First, dey steal my homelan. Den, dey stole my mama an my Goga. Ugly Crooked Teeth stole my body. Now, I'm wastin in dis daggum slave situashun. I know, the preacher say we ain't sposed to hate accordin to de Good Book, but I hate white people!

Watching Anthony walk down the long lane toward Winchester left Judah with feelings of dread. She closed her eyes and lowered her head into clasped hands.

"Dear Lawd, please watch ovah Anthony. Proteck him from de han of de enemy, de bullwhip of dem evil white folk. Bring im back to us at de appointed time, safe and unhurt. Please, Lawd Jesus. Amen."

She didn't feel the peace she typically felt after praying and, still looking down the lane, worried once again about Anthony's temper.

I caint think bout what he do if dey keep pushin im so.

She watched as he passed by the cornfield and swore she saw him stop and smell an ear of corn.

I neva heard bout nobody smellin no cohn. He walkin like he ain't got a care in de world.

She marked his steps in her mind. He says he's happy, but after last night's talk, she knew in his heart, he wasn't.

He bout to bust.

-25-

A nthony arrived early Saturday evening, having run most the way from Winchester. Opening the door, he was nearly tackled by Truelove.

"Glad you is heah. Doan you go one step fuhtha. De baby comin soon."

Wasn't but a few minutes until Anthony heard the first cries, the door opening and Truelove beaming.

"Well, c'mon in, Papa."

Born on September 1, 1827, Westley was Judah's eighth child, the fifth with Anthony. Although visibly weak, Judah smiled at her husband.

"Oh Anthony, yo heah."

"I loves you, Judah."

Anthony hugged and kissed his wife, then held Westley, barely a few minutes old.

"An dis one big baby," he beamed.

It was the first time Anthony had been home for the birth of his child.

* * * *

After three days to recover, Judah slowly walked back

to work.

"What is that terrble smell?"

There was an awful stench in the air, Judah's nose burning from the acrid smell of metal smoke. The stench was so sharp that it bit at the hairs in her nose.

Judah see-sawed back into the house.

"Oh my Lawd! What is dat?"

She followed an odor into the slop kitchen and the smell assaulted her nostrils again. She sniffed around the room looking for the source that smelled like death. She found it.

Before going into labor, she had been making hog head cheese. The pig had been butchered and had been soaking in a tub of water for more than a week. Judah had thanked the Lord that the butcher had removed the pig's eyes, brains, ears, and face, but she had to stir the tub every day to remove the excess mold and fuzz from the head skimming the top of the water with the strainer. She had planned to enlist someone to take over the stirring of the tub but went into labor and totally forgot.

She spun around and there were other foaming vats with funky meat, the smell of blood from butchering, fish guts, and rotting vegetables.

That wasn't all.

"Good Lawd!"

The blowing wind caused Judah to get a whiff of her own aroma.

"Whew! I need to go down to de crick."

* * * *

Judah had become frustrated by the talk from other slaves about how easy her life was in the manor house. She hated how they created a pecking order.

We all slaves. What we fightin ovah?

They didn't see all the work she had to do. Every day, sometimes twice a day, she had to lift the big pots full of water from the well and carry wood to keep the fire stoked... even when she was pregnant.

The other slaves didn't know the constant pressure she encountered. And she never got a break from the watchful eyes of Miss Ann and Master Hite. Even the Hites' young children seemed to be watching her every move, threatening to tell their mother or father if she did anything they did not approve.

She kept on cooking.

It what I do.

That said, Master Hite demanded that his meals be on time. Judah would wake up before the field workers and long before the rooster. Honestly, she didn't mind the work, but what she did mind was when Miss Ann, at a whim, hosted a fancy party and ordered Judah to cook a feast. She was already responsible for cooking for more than 100 people every day.

And they didn't care how tired Judah might be. If the white folks got a taste for something, Miss Ann was quick to say, "Don't worry, Judah will fix that right up." Then, at the end of the night, Miss Ann would accept all the praise for the food.

It was the same for Truelove. Miss Ann kept her running up and down the stairs to get whatever the guests wanted.

*Po Truelove workin her fingers to de bone waitin on
dem folk.*

Furthermore, the other slaves didn't have to worry
about keeping little children away from the fire every
second of every day either. If one of the slaves got sick or
hurt with a cut or rash, they'd run to Judah for healing.
Judah never said anything disparaging about the workers
in the field.

*I know it hahd work. I see de bundahs of wheat dey be
pickin an liftin. Dey de first ones wit dey lips tooted out
lookin for a sip a de tonic. Dey say, "Oh, Miss Judah, you
is so good!" Dey doan even want to talk about de nights
I spent fixin up salves an ointments. Dey used up half
my lard makin ointments wit lavender an sassafrass an
sage.*

Judah would have been satisfied if rather than saying how "good" a life she had, they would have just said
"thank you" and kept on going. Or maybe if one of the
strong men would take care of putting the house scraps
into the outdoor burning pit.

*Ain't no need comparin whose life is de worst. We all
slaves. We all got it de worst.*

* * * *

When the black preacher showed up that week, march-
ing up the road like he was on a mission, the slave folk
were hanging around the quarters on their off time.
Everyone was surprised to see him.

The preacher always carried the Good Book with him,
but Judah couldn't figure out why. She suspected he did

not know how to read, probably just wanted to look the part of a learned man. He turned the pages and made it look like he was reading but everyone knew he was just faking it and quoting the Scriptures he had heard in service. Still, he was a walking Bible.

He always talkin bout de Word from de Lawd.

Judah would soon learn the colored preacher's mission. He gathered everyone close to him that day and quietly spoke.

"Wen de niggahs go round singin 'Steal Away to Jesus,' dat mean dere goin be a ligious meetin dat night."

Master Hite didn't take too kindly to surprise visits from anybody, especially a colored man. And he certainly would not approve of a religious meeting for the enslaved.

Less he be doin all de talkin.

So, naturally, it was a secret religious meeting—the colored folks would slip off at night down into the bottoms or somewhere out of sight. Sometimes those gathered would sing and pray all night long, occasionally drumming quietly. Judah carried one of her pie baking tins as a substitute for a tambourine. Although she kept her tins at a musical whisper, for Judah it felt like being home.

Judah didn't get completely wrapped up in the Spirit like some of the others. She recalled Reverend Hite saying that "the Book of Mark 14:38 says 'watch as well as pray'" and that is exactly what she did.

I's scared de Revum Mastah gonna find us fo sho.

-26-

I n the spring of 1829, there was plenty of fuss around the plantation. Miss Ann had Truelove perfecting the main dining room, cleaning and preparing all day. It would soon be Easter.

"Truelove, this silver must sparkle," said Miss Ann. "I don't want to see a spot on any piece."

Miss Ann had Judah boil eggs so that the children could color them. Judah wasn't sure what colored eggs had to do with the death of the Lord Jesus, but she did as she was told. Judah had an easier load while the family fasted for Lent, but that changed quickly.

Dey gots me cookin enuff vittles to feed de ho world.

The butchers brought in a lamb they'd recently killed. This did make sense to Judah since she had heard Reverend Hite say Jesus died as the "Lamb of the World." Following the reverend's Passover story, Judah boiled some kale and didn't use season so they'd be bitter greens like in the story. She also stirred potatoes, tomatoes, and string beans in the skillet to make sweet treats for dessert.

The Hite family believed in looking their finest on special occasions. Miss Ann even gave Judah and the other workers their yearly clothing allotment early so they could also look the part. Judah appreciated the thought but, by late Saturday night, was angry and worried that Anthony had not returned home.

How could dey keep him slavin on de day Lawd Jesus come back to life?

Her mind again began to stray, fearful that Anthony didn't have the power to withstand slaving life much longer.

I know what he tell me, but he may be considerin runnin away. I wanna think he'd jes come heah to hide, but dat be kinda crazy for him to do. Master Hite find him, he gon beat im bad an still send im back to dat otha place.

* * * *

Early Easter Sunday, the Hite caravan ushered to the church house. Everyone traveled in formation—Reverend Hite and his family in the wagon and each class of servants by station. It looked like a grand parade.

The Hites weren't the only ones in their finest clothes that day. It seemed to Judah as if all the white folk got dressed up for Easter. The women were adorned with the prettiest hats and bonnets; the little girls wearing white gloves with ribbons on their dresses and bows in their hair. As the organ bellowed out its sound, the white people piled into the church. Even the outside audience was larger than usual.

Judah was surprised when they called for Miss Ann to sing a special song. She had no idea the Missus could sing.

"Christ the Lord is risen today, Alleluia!
Earth and heaven in chorus say, Alleluia!
Raise your joys and triumphs high, Alleluia!
Sing, ye heavens, and earth reply, Alleluia!"

Miss Ann's singing certainly stirred up the Spirit. The church became so riled up that it felt somewhat like the slaves' secret religious meetings.

Dem folks cryin somethin awful. Dey ain't gonna be time for Revum Mastah to preach.

But, after a long while, Judah saw through the window Reverend Hite standing up behind the big white box.

"Good morning, saints. Happy Resurrection Day! It's so good to see so many faces in the church today . . . especially those we haven't seen since our Christmas service."

Walking down from the pulpit, he continued, "Sister Sarah, that smile on your face under that big hat tells me that these strapping young men lining this pew are all your sons joining their Mama for Easter."

"Yes, indeed, Pastor. Thank the Good Lord." Sarah wiped her brow underneath the hat's brim with her white handkerchief.

"Let me see who else is here on the Lord's Day. Oh my goodness! Elijah, is that you?"

The smile on the reverend's face lit up the room. Judah could even see it from outside on the lawn.

"Ladies and gentlemen, this young man is the grandson of one of my oldest and dearest friends from the war, Francis Lovejoy from Maine. And his daddy, Daniel, is a Congregational minister. Let me introduce you to Elijah Lovejoy. He's a Northerner, but we won't hold that against him, will we church?"

"No, sir," the white folks called out in laughter.

"Brother, what are you doing here? Your letter said you weren't coming in until Thursday."

"I just wanted to surprise you. I hope that's okay."

"Okay? It's wonderful," said Reverend Hite, giving Elijah a hearty hug.

Remembering where he was, he turned back to the congregation.

"Oh, I'm sorry, y'all. Elijah's grandfather was like an older brother to me, but distance and time does not matter because we are all family in the Lord."

"Amen," rang the congregation.

Reverend Hite didn't take much time to let the congregation's feelings simmer down. He kept preaching.

"My message today is meant to show you that our spiritual freedom came at a high price and that we should take up our cross and follow the One who provided that freedom for us!

Hite resumed his place behind the pulpit.

"In the book of Philippians, the Apostle Paul describes Jesus' great love for us. He says that Jesus didn't think of himself so highly that he couldn't become like us. Though he was God, he did not think of equality with God as something to cling to. Instead, he gave up his divine privileges; he took the humble position being born as a human being. When he appeared in human form, he humbled himself in obedience to God and died a criminal's death on a cross. Therefore, God elevated him to the place of highest honor and gave him the name above all other names. You've got to understand that at the name of Jesus every knee will bow, in heaven and on earth and under the earth, and every tongue shall confess that Jesus Christ is Lord, to the glory of God the Father."

Judah noticed heads bobbing in agreement.

"I want to turn your attention to the topic of freedom. As Americans, we must accept that God means us to be free. The Founding Fathers started this country so that we could have the right to be free. Jesus came so that we could be free!"

"Amen!"

He continued his sermon.

"The Liberty Bell is a treasured symbol of the early days of American independence. The inscription on the bell reads 'Proclaim Liberty throughout all the land unto all the inhabitants thereof' and that, my friends, is from Leviticus 25:10. This bell is a great symbol that stirs our national hearts with pride. However, there is a symbol for all eternity that outlives and outshines all symbols of every nation—The Cross of Christ. Thank you, Jesus!"

Hite put his glasses on the end of his nose and said, "Turn with me to Matthew 27 and we'll start reading from verse 31."

"And after that they had mocked him, they took the robe off from him, and put his own raiment on him, and led him away to crucify him. And as they came out, they found a man of Cyrene, Simon by name: him they compelled to bear his cross. And when they were come unto a place called Golgotha, a place of a skull, they gave him vinegar to drink mingled with gall. And when he had tasted thereof, he would not drink. And they crucified him and parted his garments."

The reverend looked up and the crowd stopped reading.

"You see, this Simon of Cyrene was a nigra. His job was to carry the cross of Jesus. Maybe that was God's way of showing us the value of negro labor?"

Judah felt the eyes of the congregation looking out the windows at the darker group sitting outside. To Judah, it was like they all said at the same time, "See, y'all is right where you belong!"

Hite continued.

"Paul tells us that both Jews and Gentiles have been united by the death of Christ on the Cross. The empty tomb reveals that we can be raised from the deadness of our sin and can live in the power of His resurrection! The Bible says that Jesus cried out from the cross and the veil in the temple ripped from the bottom to the top. You know why that's important?"

The congregation wanted to know.

"Well, they say that veil, the curtain, was four inches thick. If horses were tied to it, even they couldn't pull it apart. The veil barred all but the High Priest from the presence of God, but when it was torn in two at the death of Jesus of Nazareth, access to God was made available to all who come through him. The Bible says that there was a great earthquake and the rocks were rent and graves opened up and the dead walked free. Free!

"When the people saw this, they cried out, 'Truly this was the Son of God!' Primarily the symbols of Christianity are simple; a wooden cross and an empty tomb. However, these symbols are meaningless unless we find our own personal freedom from bondage through them. Because of a simple wooden cross, we know our sins can be forgiven. Because of an empty tomb, we have hope for our eternal self! Christ came to save us! Only one man died for our sins, was buried in a tomb and came out of that tomb three days later. Jesus came to give us eternal liberty. He came that you might have life and have it more abundantly. For those who are saved, this is a moment that fills our hearts with thankfulness and gratitude. For those needing deliverance, it is a moment of revelation that Christ came to set you free!

"John 8:36 says, 'If the Son therefore shall make you free, ye shall be free indeed.' Stand to your feet."

The piano began to play, and a white lady stood to sing.

> "Alas! and did my Savior bleed
> and did my Sovereign die! Would
> He devote that sacred head for
> sinners such as I?"

After the benediction, the people filed out of the church in a row as the woman sang. Master stood at the bottom of the stairs and holy hugged and kissed everyone as they walked out. She was still singing as Elijah Lovejoy took his turn.

"Reverend Hite, it was so good to see you up there. You are in your element."

"Elijah, you are a breath of fresh air for sure."

"Funny," said Elijah. "I want to call you Major Hite, like my granddad always did."

"God rest his soul," said Isaac. "Goodness, last time Ann and I saw you was just after you graduated from college."

"Five years ago . . . I was looking to be somewhere away

from Maine."

"So, you end up in Missouri. Your letter mentioned that you run a school."

"It's a challenge, but I love it. Although, between you and me, I am thinking of furthering my own education to become a Presbyterian minister."

"That is wonderful to hear," said Reverend Hite as his wife walked up beside him.

"Elijah, so happy to see you again."

"Sister Hite, I hope I'm not imposing."

"Not at all," said Miss Ann. "There's always room for you and we have plenty to go around. I hope you brought your appetite."

"Thank you, my lady."

Except for being in his late twenties, Elijah Lovejoy didn't look that special to Judah, just another white man.

* * * *

It took a while after the benediction for all the white folks to finish hugging each other before the Hites could leave the church. Prince, the cab driver, held out his hand for Miss Ann to mount the wagon while the reverend walked around to the other side.

"Take us home, Prince," commanded Master Hite and the caravan took off for Belle Grove, the line of slaves looking like worker ants leaving the nest.

"Mastah all a-pep chattin up dis Lovejoy fella," Judah told Truelove.

When the procession took the turn that led to the plantation, Judah didn't feel the dread she usually felt. She imagined that Master would be in a good mood with his friend around.

On Tuesday evening, Isaac told Ann he and Elijah were going to have dinner at Wilkerson Tavern, a stone's throw down the road from Belle Grove. When Judah heard about the plans, she surmised Master Hite didn't want his wife fussing at him while he and young Lovejoy were drinking. They certainly weren't going to find a better meal.

I's sho Lovejoy know that by now as much as he et on Sunday.

Judah was cleaning up the kitchen when the men returned from the tavern. She knew by the ruckus they had enjoyed too much to drink. From the listening post, Judah heard Mr. Lovejoy fussing at Master Hite.

"Isaac, I don't understand how you can still be in this slavery business. It's a shame before God. Exodus 21:16 says 'And he that stealeth a man, and selleth him, or if he be found in his hand, he shall surely be put to death.' How can you, a man of the cloth, be convinced that this is right? Do you believe that stuff you preach about?"

"Of course, I do. God's word is precious and sharing the gospel is the most important thing I do."

"You can't believe that, Isaac."

"What do you mean, Elijah? I take my ministry duties seriously. The Lord Jesus told us to 'feed his sheep' and that is exactly what I do."

"I sat in that church on Easter Sunday and heard you crank out that sermon on 'freedom in Christ.' You even quoted John 8:36 'If the Son therefore shall make you free, you shall be free indeed.'"

"That's right. What's your point, Elijah?"

"I just can't understand how you can preach all that freedom and liberty stuff and have this house full of slaves!"

"What are you talking about?"

"I'm talking about you preaching to all those folks about Jesus' love setting people free; and all the while, you had those poor negroes sitting on the lawn. Now, I'll ask you again, do you really believe what you preach about?"

"Elijah, I'm not doubting you've been brought up reading the Bible, but where is this all coming from?"

"I abhor the slave trade, and I make it my duty to address myself to you personally. I am coming to you as a brother in that spirit of meekness and humility that becomes a follower of the Lamb, and at the same time with all that boldness and sincerity of speech which should mark the language of a freeman and a Christian. It is not my design or wish to offend, but simply to maintain my rights as a republican citizen, free-born of these United States, and to defend, fiercely, the cause of truth and righteousness. I believe slavery is an abomination against God."

"Elijah, you have been at my house for four days eating my food prepared by my slaves and sleeping comfortably on a bed made up by those same slaves. Now you've got some sort of righteous indignation?"

"I've got a little secret for you, Isaac. I haven't slept comfortably all week! I've been sleeping on the floor just so not to mess up the bed that your slaves have been ordered to make. And, I admit it, it's true, Judah's cooking is the best I've had in a very long time, but, Isaac, it's wrong! God's children should not be treated that way. They should not be just let out to work. They're people, for God's sake!"

Master Hite raged, "People? They were born to breed

and work; nothing more, nothing less."

"Whom the Son sets free is free indeed," said Lovejoy.

"Cursed be Canaan," countered Hite, "a servant of servants shall he be unto his brethren. Genesis 9:25."

"Isaac, do you really believe the Lord would honor a curse made by an old drunk? Tell me something. How can churchgoing, Bible-worshipping, Jesus-loving Christians justify the practice of owning another human being?"

"'Slaves, obey your masters in all things according to the flesh.' That's Colossians 3:22. 'Slaves, obey your earthly masters with fear and trembling' . . . Ephesians 6:5. 'Slaves, submit to your masters' . . . Titus 2:9. Face it, Elijah, God supports owning slaves!"

"You just got done preaching about Christ's liberty. Did you forget Jesus in the temple reading from the book of Isaiah? He said he was come to set at liberty those who were captive. How do you justify slavery; this blatant bigotry?"

"Bigotry? You make me laugh, Elijah. 'God cursed Ham and his descendants forever.' Those descendants are the dark-skinned people in Africa where these slaves come from. God himself justified owning servants. On Mount Sinai, God gave his commandments—his law—and talked about the 'maid-servant' or 'man-servant' in the same sentence where he referred to the ox and the ass as property to be purchased. God's champions, Abraham and Peter, talk about owning servants. We are doing God's work here. If we didn't bring the light of God's love to that dark continent, just imagine how evil it would be."

"Imagine how it would be if we never interfered," argued Lovejoy. "You know we whites aren't the only

Christians and that there are blacks in the New Testament. You said it yourself. The man, Simon the Cyrene, who carried Jesus' cross to Calvary was a black man. In the Book of Acts, Barnabus and the Apostle Paul were sent on their missionary journey by Simeon. The Bible is sure to point out that some called him 'niger.' Sound familiar?"

Lovejoy paused, but only to clear his throat.

"It seems to me," he continued, "that the very nature of God would be opposed to one human being owning another in any situation. Slavery of Africans is an incredible stain and atrocity on the human race when slavery exists in any culture! Isaac, in the name of God, set these people free!"

I could be set free from this hearth I been chained to all dese years.

It was quiet for the longest time. Judah imagined Master grabbing his big family Bible and turning the pages fiercely. But he could also quote Scripture from memory.

"Leviticus 25:44 says that 'Both thy bondmen, and thy bondmaids, which thou shalt have, shall be of the heathen that are round about you; of them shall ye buy bondmen and bondmaids. Moreover, of the children of the strangers that do sojourn among you, of them shall ye buy, and of their families that are with you, which they begat in your land: and they shall be your possession. And ye shall take them as an inheritance for your children after you, to inherit them for a possession; they shall be your bondmen forever: but over your brethren the children of Israel, ye shall not rule one over another with rigor.' I intend to keep my slaves and will pass them on to my children as their inheritance. It is my right."

"The Golden Rule, Isaac, treat others as you would wish them to treat you."

"You are nothing more than an abolitionist," Hite snapped, obviously agitated.

"I am indeed, Isaac, if you are defining abolition to mean freedom from slavery."

Mebbe dere is some good white people in this world afta awl.

"I'm going to bed," Hite bellowed. "When I wake up, I expect that all this nonsense talk will be done. Goodnight, Elijah."

"I'm not done, Isaac. You can't tell me being a slaver hasn't changed you. I've seen the effects of this practice in trade. It changes people. You're a man of the cloth. This institution is sinful and ungodly. I've seen good people get caught up with the power of it all. I'll even bet you've done things you would have never done before. Got these poor folks running around calling you master. Did you forget the Bible says in Matthew 6:24 'No man can serve two masters'?"

"Goodnight, Elijah." Judah heard Master Hite's foot-steps move across the room.

"Just one more question, Isaac. In all that preaching you do about heaven, have you ever considered whether those colored souls are welcomed in heaven?"

"Of course, they are welcome. Elijah, our Lord Jesus decreed in John the fourteenth chapter 'In my Father's house are many mansions.' Who else is going to clean all those rooms?" Reverend Hite chuckled as he considered his own cleverness.

The conversation between the old friends continued, Judah sitting in her spot at the bottom of the steps, locked up tight in a ball as she listened.

"Even the constitution of the United States of America," Lovejoy proclaimed, "states that all men are created equal."

"C'mon Elijah, you know those very men who wrote those words were slavers themselves, so obviously they weren't talking or thinking about the slaves. They were talkin' about white people, white men in particular."

"And that's not bigotry? What about the abuses that the masters enact against the enslaved? God disallows such ill treatment. And, it is what causes slaves to revolt."

"I really do need to get some sleep, Elijah."

"Isaac, on top of it all, slavery is an evil borne of the devil. The immorality of slavery denies the godliness in all mankind. God created us all. He made us all one. Galatians 3:28 'there is neither Jew nor Greek, there is neither slave nor free, there is neither male nor female: for ye are all one in Christ Jesus.' I cannot surrender my principles even if the whole world should vote them down. I can make no compromise between truth and error, even though my life be the alternative."

The men went back and forth with each other for hours, neither willing to concede. For a while, Judah thought they were about to come to fisticuffs. Several times, their voices turned very loud. Master always argued loud, especially when he'd been drinking whiskey.

"Isaac, I do wish you would reconsider your point. There's a curse awaiting the white plantation class."

"Elijah, God is white. Jesus is white. God put white folks

on this planet to conquer and rule. Who's going to curse us?"

"Jesus was born in Israel. The Bible said he had hair like lamb's wool and feet like bronze. What white man do you know that looks like that?"

When Judah awoke the following day, her heart sang "woke up dis mornin wit my min stayed on freedom."

She didn't dare sing it out loud.

-27-

J udah, at times, wearied of mothering all her babies, but she couldn't seem to help herself when Anthony was around. By late 1829, she was big again.

At least the children were quite helpful in the kitchen.

Sam and George, however, had been assigned fulltime work. Almost 16, Sam was learning the building and general repair trade from his father. Master Hite even allowed him to sometimes travel to other plantations when Anthony was on loan. Sam was thrilled, his mother only approving because it might keep Anthony from losing his temper again.

George also was happy to be learning a trade, mentored by Daniel and Emmanuel to become a blacksmith. Hard work, but certainly better than laboring in the field from sunrise to sunset.

Now 13, Marcus was showing signs of manhood, teaching the toddlers in the family how to properly pick ripe vegetables from the garden when he wasn't retrieving wood, fetching water pots, or being assigned duties away from the kitchen by Master Hite.

Milly and Mary took turns terrorizing the younger kids. One day they dragged Anthony to the flour bin. Within seconds, he was covered white.

Young Anthony was not pleased, but the girls found it hilarious.

"Mama, we gots a new mastah . . . Lil Anthony."

While Judah had an urge to join the fun, she was more worried the Hites would walk in unannounced.

On March 16, 1830, Elias became the ninth child in the family. Unfortunately, Anthony was unable to meet his new baby until he was four days old.

* * * *

Judah was out in the garden picking tomatoes; they were getting heavy on the vine. She stood up to wipe the sweat from her brow and noticed a strange black figure coming down the road. She couldn't quite see who it was, just the shape of a man. She could tell it was an older man by the way he walked—not tall and upright—but proud. He was dressed like he was going to church. The figure kept walking and Judah kept staring.

"Miss Judah, whatchu lookin at?" Truelove called from the doorway.

"I dunno. Somebody comin down de way."

Truelove stepped outside to get a look.

"Lawd today, dat be ol Manuel! He use to be on dis plantashun when I was a youngin. Use to work in de stable takin care uv de hawses. Mastah Hite set him free while back."

As Manuel approached the manor house, Truelove stepped away from the garden to meet him. Manuel saw Truelove coming and took off his hat and nodded his head toward her like a gentleman. "Miss Truelove, it sho' is good to see you."

Truelove smiled a big grin. "Manuel, whatchu doin here?" She seemed genuinely happy to see him and equally confused by his presence.

"I'm here to see Revum Martster bout Emmanuel." Manuel looked off into the direction of the barn. "How my boy? He doin all right? He been mindin Master Hite?"

"Oh, yo son jes fine. He a good boy. Ain't no trouble at all. He a big boy now, tall an strong. He do de work of a team of hawses."

Judah just stood there taking it all in, trying not to call attention to herself. It looked like the two were having a family reunion. Out of the corner of her eye, Truelove noticed Judah.

"Lawd, where my mannahs at? Judah, dis here Manuel. He Emmanuel's daddy. Manuel, dis be Miss Judah, de finest cook we evah had at Belle Grove."

Judah wiped her hand on her apron and stretched it out to him.

"Happy to meet you, Mistah Manuel. I'm sorry my hands be a lil dirty from wuhkin de gahden."

Manuel smiled a toothless grin and extended his hand back at Judah.

"Dat doan make me no nevah mind, Miss Judah. A pleasah to meet you too."

"You hungry, Mistah Manuel? I think I gots a few biscuits left from breakfast. An I could slice up summa dese maters I jes picked. You's welcome to it."

"Dat's right kind a you, Miss Judah. I's not too hungry, but I's not one to turn down a good meal an Truelove here seem to be vouchin fo yo cookin. I'd be a fool to miss out. Thank you, ma'am."

"Let me go in de kitchen an wrestle up some vittles. Woan take but a minute." Judah hustled into the house carrying the tomato basket on her hip.

Judah must have been causing a stir with her hurrying about the kitchen, slicing and plating. She hadn't heard Master Hite enter through the screen door.

"Judah, what's going on? You look like you're putting on a big to-do. Miss Ann expecting guests or something for supper?"

Judah stopped cutting up vegetables on the table for a moment. "Nossah, Master Hite. You do gots a visitah here, though."

"A visitor? Who's here?"

"Ol Mistah Manuel heah. Truelove say he useta wuhk fo you a whiles back. I's jes puttin togetha a plate a vittles to show him dat naybullie kinness like you teach us."

"Manuel's here? I wonder what he wants."

I doan think I evah seen Revum Master look confused an suhprised like he do now.

"I'm going to go talk to him," said Master Hite.

It was just a few seconds before Judah followed with Mister Manuel's food.

"Emmanuel Jackson, as I live and breathe. What are you doing here? Welcome home. How have you been? Come on and set down, Old Timer. Take a load off."

"Thank you, Revum Hite."

Manuel's bones creaked as he sat down on the ground. As she set a plate of food next to the visitor, Judah marked Hite's apparent discomfort with Manuel being so informal.

Manuel took a bite out of the biscuit. "Mmm, delishus!" He looked up toward Judah. "Miss Judah, Truelove ain't lie. Dese biscuits is so tasty. Thank ya, kindly."

Seeing those gums again, this time enjoying her food, made Judah smile. Manuel took an even bigger bite the next time. He didn't even finish chewing before he got down to his business.

"Massah . . . I'm sorry, Revum Hite. I come to talk to you bout my boy."

"Emmanuel, Jr.? What about him?"

"It's jes that . . . I wuz wonderin if'n you'd be willin to give him his freedom like you did wit me?"

"Freedom for Emmanuel, Jr.? That's a whole different story. I gave you manumission because you were getting too old to keep up the work. Emmanuel is a strong young man. He's a great help here on the farm. I'd be losing a lot if I lost him."

"I know I's askin a lot. I's willin to buy him from you. I been workin as I'm able an I've saved up quite a few dollahs. Mebbe we can work out a fair price soze you ain't losin out."

Master Hite's jaw about dropped out his skull. "You want to buy your own son?"

"Yessuh, I do. If'n you an Miss Ann will sell him to me."

"Diddy, Is dat you?" Young Emmanuel ran up from the barn with a big smile on his face, showing every tooth in his mouth. He grabbed hold of his papa and swung him around like a child's rag doll.

"Diddy, I's so happy to see you! I ain't know if'n you wuz livin or daid." Tears welled up in his eyes as he talked.

"How you been gettin along?"

"I been fair to middlin, if I'm bein honest."

"But, whatchu doin here at Belle Grove?"

"I's sorry. Dis ain't no social call. I got some bidness to tend to wid de Revum Hite."

"Judah, Truelove, let's go inside and leave these two to talk," said Master Hite. As they walked away from father and son, Judah looked back to see the two Emmanuels going over the hill toward the barn.

Mebbe young Emmanuel wanna show his papa what he bin wuhkin on in de blacksmith shop.

Later, old Manuel came up to Master Hite, sitting in his cane chair on the front porch.

"Revum Hite, I's sorry to come callin unannounced."

"It's not a problem, Emmanuel. Belle Grove is always open to you. And by the way, if you can raise $800, I am willing to part with Emmanuel. Do you think you can raise that?"

"Dat's a steep price. It might take me a while. I have some money stowed up, but if you is willin to cept paymints, I think I kin save up de rest."

"Well, you get the money and this offer is good. No matter how long it takes. And I will accept payments. You've always been an honest and hard worker."

Toothless Manuel grinned again.

"Oh, thank you, Revum Hite. You mades me a happy man."

The old man wandered down the lane just like he had come.

-28-

On a hot afternoon in August 1831, Judah heard Master Hite screaming upstairs.

"Ann, listen to this. Right here in *The Virginian,* it says some slaves revolted and killed nearly 60 white people over in Southampton County."

"Oh, my goodness," Miss Ann shrieked.

"They are looking for the nigger leader named Nat Turner. Paper describes him as 'Five feet six or eight inches high, weighs between 150 and 160 pounds, rather bright and light-colored complexion, but not a mulatto, broad shoulders, large flat nose, large eyes, broad flat feet, rather knock-kneed, walks brisk and active, hair on the top of the head very thin, no beard, except on the upper lip and the top of the chin, a scar on one of his temples, also one on the back of his neck, a large knot on one of the bones of his right arm, near the wrist, produced by a blow.' Oh, they'll catch him."

"I hope they get that dreadful nigger soon, Isaac. He sounds frightening. And I hope they catch every nigger responsible and execute them all."

From that point on, Master joined in with his wife's suspicion of the slaves. He even hired more overseers to help keep an eye on the plantation.

Unlike many plantations, the Hites only occasionally employed overseers. Reverend Hite preferred his own hands-on approach to handling his enslaved population. He simply assigned various tasks to do in a day. Whenever the Hites left Belle Grove, Master Hite would leave the workforce with orders that had better be completed when he returned.

Watching this new group of strange white men, Judah worried about her girls.

Crooked Teeth, Mastah Shields, dat slave brokah fella. Deys all ovah de place.

-29-

A s always on a Sunday morning, the enslaved sat on the grass outside the church. Judah listened to Reverend Hite preach about God's love and loving your neighbor. She'd been listening to that for more than twenty years. Today, though, she really listened, and she questioned.

Who was dis God that let his dark creations be treated like dis? If he so lovin, I say, what bout de slaves? Would a lovin God let my chillun rot in slavery all dey lives and get passed round Mastah's family like dis some game? If he so good and he so lovin, why did he let dose white men kill off all our elders an destroy Goga and ship me here? Why? To die? Why he let ol Crooked Teeth do me dat way? Dat caint be de same God Revum Mastah talkin bout. Mebbe dere's a diffent God for us colored folk?

Following Sunday service, the Hite clan made the turn to go down the lane at Belle Grove. Judah's eyes lit upon Elijah Lovejoy standing on the front steps by the columns. Reverend Hite stood up in the wagon.

"Elijah? What are you doing here? This is a pleasant surprise. I wasn't expecting you." Isaac jumped down from the wagon to greet his friend.

"I hope you are planning to stay for lunch. I'm sure Judah's made plenty."

Hmmpf! I take dat as an insult. A course dere's plenty to eat. Dere's always enough, even when dere ain't enough.

"I don't want to impose, Isaac."

Lovejoy's humbleness was a refreshing sight. To Judah, such humility was unusual for the whites.

"Don't be preposterous. No imposition at all. Come on into the house. I'm sure lunch will be ready shortly."

Master Hite looked in Judah's direction and squinted his eyes as if to say, "I better be right."

Judah served pork and gravy with rice. She added pickled cucumbers into a salad with onions. She hadn't planned to serve pickles that day, but the surprise guest made it necessary to have enough food on the table. Truelove also brought out plenty of rum and whiskey for the men to drink. When things started to slow down a bit, Truelove and Judah took their places at the bottom of the stairs.

It took but a moment to realize what the white men were discussing.

"So, what have you been up to since your last visit?" asked Isaac. "How many years has it been?"

"Easter of '29," said Elijah. "And I have been busy these past four years. I'm proud to say that I studied at Princeton Theological Seminary in New Jersey and am now an ordained Presbyterian minister."

"Well, that's wonderful, Elijah."

"And I also have established and am the editor of the *St. Louis Observer*, a weekly Presbyterian newspaper."

"I'd love to see some of your writings," said Isaac.

"I will definitely send you a couple. Let me warn ahead of time they are strongly against slavery, church denominations that uphold that sin, and President Jackson."

"Elijah, I don't want to hear this today. I think we covered it in full last time we spoke and my position has not changed."

"I just don't want you to continue in sin, Isaac. The stain of oppression is going to bring God's judgment to America. What kind of friend would I be if I didn't tell you the truth?"

Judah and Truelove heard Miss Ann excuse herself, saying "men's talk was no place for womenfolk."

The two friends continued to drink, but their talk didn't get as heated as the last time. Somehow their conversation turned to the virtues of living in the big city of St. Louis as opposed to Middletown, Virginia. Judah soon grew tired of their nonsense talk. She wanted Reverend Lovejoy to speak more about abolition. After a while, she decided to go back into the kitchen to clean things up and start the evening meal.

As she focused on preparations, Judah was shaken by the presence of Reverend Lovejoy in her kitchen.

"Judah, I want to talk to you for a moment."

Not knowing how to react to a visitor in her area, she immediately worried about Master Hite's reaction.

"You get enough to eat, Revum Lovejoy? Can I fix you somethin?"

"Oh my, yes. I'm afraid I have glutted myself."

He paused and looked her in the eyes.

"Listen, I don't have much time to explain. Isaac fell

asleep. He never could hold his liquor."

Ain't dat de truth.

"Judah, I want to speak with you about your condition. I know a way to get you off this plantation to your freedom."

Dere's dat word agin . . . freedom.

"I have some friends who could get you on the railroad."

"I ain't nevah been on no train befo, sir. I's nervous bout dat."

He hushed his voice.

"The railroad isn't a train at all. It's a group of people who are committed to helping the enslaved escape their plantations to find freedom in the north in a place called Canada. Not all white folks approve of slavery and some of us are devoted to ending it. If we need to help every single slave escape to end it, then so be it."

"But I caint escape. I gots ten chillun heah and my husband heah, too. I jes caint leave em. Mebbe we can figger out how to get my chillun free first an den I'll leave wit you on dis railroad. My oldest boys is probly de strongest to make de trip. Mebbe get dem to freedom fuhst."

"Okay, send us whoever you choose. Watch the sky. When the North Star is the brightest, that will be your signal. Your boys will have to be ready. We won't have time for dawdling. Listen closely . . ."

He leaned closer and pointed a stern finger in Judah's face.

"You must not tell anyone what I've talked about today, not even your husband or children until it's time. Your life and my life could be in danger if anyone finds out what we are doing."

"Yessuh . . . I mean, nossuh. No one will know."

Lovejoy hurried back upstairs, and Judah was suddenly overwhelmed by nerves. She couldn't tell if her anxiety was related to being able to put her trust in this white man or if Master Hite would catch on to their escape plan.

The Lord must have known about Reverend Lovejoy's plans. It wasn't long after Elijah Lovejoy headed north that Master Hite walked into the kitchen with Emily, Mary's child.

"Judah, I brought Emily here to help you in the kitchen. We have gotten bigger here and we are feeding many more servants than before. My hope is that you will show her how to be a cook. And she can help you with cleaning and other tasks, as well. Perhaps she can be of use to you."

"Thank you, Master Hite. I am indeed grateful."

"Emily, you is my boy George's age? Dat right?"

"Sixteen, Miss Judah."

"I's even youngah when I stahted in de kitchen. I's so glad to have you heah."

Judah was not going to treat Emily like Aunt Sally had treated her. Sally had thought Judah too young to be any help and had complained Judah was "too wet hind de eahs." Now, with what Judah knew about running a kitchen, she would admit that Sally was right.

I ain't had no bidness in de kitchen; I prolly should have been out pickin tobacky leaves.

"I got lots to teach you, gal. Jes listen to what I gots to say and doan gets in my way."

Judah paused, realizing she was sounding more like Aunt Sally than she wanted. Judah smiled.

"If I evah seem too tuff, you jes knows dat I gonna hep

you becomes a great cook."

Dis gal young. I like dem two plaits sticking out de sides of her head like the tails on the pigs.

Judah led Emily around the kitchen. When they arrived at the winter hearth, she stopped and turned to look Emily in the face.

"Dis be de mos important room in dis entire great house. Dis is where it all happen. I feeds way mo dan one hunnered people three times a day, so dat tells you how much work I gets done in a day. You gots to be ready for bidness when you come in heah."

Judah pulled her over to the fireplace.

"Sho is hot in here, Miss Judah," said Emily, quickly taking two steps back from the fire.

"Get used to it. Dis fire burns de whole day an night, de entire year round. Summah an winnah. It nevah gets not hot in dis room."

"It be smoky too, Miss Judah." Emily barked and choked as she spoke.

"You gets use to dat too. De smoke and de heat be a necessary evil."

Emily continued to cough, backing away even more from the fire.

"Chile, get yo hin parts ovah heah and stan by dis heah fire."

"Yes, ma'am."

Emily hung her head and dragged her feet over to the stone fireplace.

"You jes stand right dere so you can learn to preciate de heat. Once we start cookin, ain't no gettin away from de powah of de flame. In de summa, this fire is jes as hot, but you caint let de fire go out. It gets so hot dat you gonna wanna sleep outside. De skeeters an hoaseflies will get you fo sho but you make yo choice . . . hot or bit. In de wintah, dis fire is your best frien. Yo toes can burn from de heat or burn from de fros. You'll be beggin to get round this fire."

Judah returned to her work, but every so often, looked over her shoulder to see Emily wiping her eyes and nose. Judah was determined not to give in to her sniveling. The longer Emily complained with tears and sobs, the longer Judah attached to the idea that Emily would stay right there.

When Judah finished with her chopping and peeling tasks, she leaned toward Emily.

"Gal, if you gon work in dis kitchen wit me, you gon have to quit all dat cryin an mess. Dis is what we gots to do. Ain't no gettin away from it."

Judah put her hand on Emily's shoulder.

"I's not tryin' to be mean, chile, but dis de life of a slave cook. It ain't easy. An honest to goodness, Master Hite seem nice, but doan mess wit dat man's vittles. He like it done when it sposed to be done an if it's not, dey gonna be hell to pay. An I ain't bout to be sponsible fo yo mistakes!"

Judah grabbed Emily's chin and inspected her skin.

Lawd, her face is hot!

"Heah, let's get you some cool watah."

The girl drank it down in one gulp.

"Miss Judah?"

"Yes, Emily?"

"How long you been at Belle Grove?"

"Chile, let me think on it."

Judah rubbed her chin. She felt three or four little stubbly hairs.

When did dose get dere?

"Pret near twenna years, I reckon. A long time. A long, long time."

Just saying the length of time made her think about her plans with Reverend Lovejoy. Judah hoped Emily couldn't see the sneaky smile come on her face.

Little do she know de part she gonna play in my scheme for freedom.

"C'mon gal, I gots much to teach you."

An not a lot of time to do it.

-30-

At the first hint of dawn, Judah was walking toward the kitchen. She stopped for a moment and looked toward the northern sky.

"Lawd," she whispered. "I caint wait to get away from here!"

She had awakened early that morning, even before the birds had stirred. She had joy in her heart and couldn't help but sing.

Westley was the first child to open an eye.

"Mama, what you so happy an singin bout?"

He rolled over and pulled his blanket up over his head.

Judah kept singing, possibly even louder.

"I sing cause I'm happy. I doan need a reason. I got love in my heart an sometimes you jes gots to let it out!"

Mary, 14-years-old and not one for waking up early, sleepily contributed a half-yawn, half-growl.

"What you gots to be so happy fo, Mama?"

"I got my life. I got y'all. I got Anthony."

George laughed.

"You got Belle Grove. You got chains an whips. Sho, you gots it all."

"You ain't gon get me down, George. What's so wrong

226

wid me bein happy?"

Judah had not told George, Sam or Marcus about the plan for them to escape. "What's so wrong wid me bein happy?"

"You just been actin so strange," said George. "Like nothin can get you down. You been singin an' hummin all de time. An Papa been up to Winchestah an den down in Woodstock. He ain't been here to make you smile. It jes strange is all."

"I ain't know my bein happy bothered y'all so bad. I'll try to be saddah from now on."

* * * *

The North Star appeared, but Judah's boys were sound asleep in the cabin. A few days earlier, George had accidentally caught his shirtsleeve in the blacksmith's fire and, in the momentary panic, dropped the hammer on his foot. He was much better, but still hobbling.

Dat boy ain't goin nowhere. Maybe Revum Lovejoy come round agin an we try it den.

-31-

It was an early summer evening in 1834, Judah cud-
dled with one-month-old Emily in the rocking chair
Anthony had made from scraps of wood he'd managed
to collect. Just in front of the cabin porch, two-year-old
Elijah, child number ten, was sitting in the dirt playing
with hand-me-down corn cobs. As the sun dropped in
blazing orange and red, Judah hitched her wrap around
her shoulders and Anthony, just home from a week in
Woodstock, began to kindle a fire. For a moment, her
mind drifted to her childhood in Goga, then back again
as she scanned her own children, reposed in the waning
sunlight as they relished having completed the chores and
work for the evening.

Goodness, the entire family was here. Judah cracked a
smile as she saw the fire glowing on the little kids' faces.

"Mama?" asked Maria. "You been on dis here plantation a long time, huh?"

"Sho nuff. I's seen many a planting season here at Belle
Grove. I done raise y'all an here we sits still. Plenny a
times I been right heah on dis porch watchin y'all runnin
all ovah de place."

"Why you cryin, Mama?" Westley worried.

228

"I's jes thinkin bout home."

"Home? Mama, you is home. Right heah at Belle Grove."

"Chile, dis ain't nevah bin my home. Dis be my home cuz I's here wit y'all, but I wasn't born no slave. In Goga, I wuz free. I went where I pleased. Only my mama an baba to hol me countable. That wuz until de white folks got dere."

Judah lifted her head.

Mama . . . Baba . . .

Judah stroked baby Emily's head. Eleven children. Age was creeping up, her strength and energy declining. What's more, she couldn't seem to shake the cough she had contracted. She presumed it came from sucking up all the smoke from the fire. She made and drank tonic by the bucket it seemed, but nothing helped. A few days earlier, while making dinner, she had coughed up some phlegm that accidentally fell in the food. She quickly stirred it into the mix, not even trying to scoop it out.

Dem white folks already stolen my yeahs, they can have a little taste of my spit.

* * * *

Truelove came down the stairs with a look of concern on her face.

"Judah, I heard Mastah talkin to Missy about givin your boy George to his son, Mastah Walker, when he turn twenny-five. Dat ain't but two yeahs from now."

Judah pulled back, silent in shock.

"No," she finally muttered.

"Dat ain't all, Judah. When Mastah Cornelius turn eighteen, the Revum Mastah gonna give im Marcus. An he promised Milly to Hugh. He think she'll be a good cook for im. He also promised Walker that he could have Lil Anthony."

"Oh, Lawd, not my chillun!"

"Dat's de way it be, Judah. You nos dat. Dey pass on our chillen to dey own chillen."

Soon, Master Hite came down the stairs and Judah rushed at him.

"Mastah, please! I tole my chillum we stay togethah until abolishun come!"

"Abolition!" His face turned red with anger. "What do you know about abolition? Ain't never gonna be no abolition! It'll take an act of war for me to free my nigras. I better not ever hear you speak of abolition again . . . you hear me?"

He reared back his hand as if he fixing to slap Judah.

"Yes, Mastah, but George an Sam been wuhkin lon side Anthony an dey could be of great hep fo you heah."

Master Hite turned away and walked back up the stairs.

"Leave it, Judah."

Judah nearly fell onto her chair, trying to cover her eyes from the explosion of tears. She had seen multiple times over the years how slave children were sold or given away and she wondered if there was any possible way to change Master Hite's mind.

Since Elijah Lovejoy's visit, Judah had secretly pined for freedom. And now, she had an official white man's word for it—abolition. She regretted letting the word slip from her mind, but more than ever she imagined life in a place where her family could be free.

Do as we please, widout no pass, widout somebody

else pahmishun. Mastah know dat I fed his chillen an grow dem strong. An now dey gonna own my chillen? Dat ain't right!

In the ensuing weeks, Judah's tolerance for being enslaved vanished.

I jes caint be satisfied to be somebody's slave no mo. I am chile of de Congo, de mighty river, not borned to be somebody's cook on some plantashun. I ain't sposed to be here. I's from de junga where de seasons is hot or hot an wet. Not dis spring, summa, fall, an winna mess. When de snow fly, all I can think bout is de sunshine on de coast. I's rather be standin on de cliffs of Mont Nabeba or catchin rainfall on my tongue in de vallies of Montenge.

Judah sat near the fireplace and the only thing on her mind was wrapping her babies close to her body and running away from Belle Grove. On a Saturday when Anthony came home from wherever he had been, they would take all the children and head north. They could hide in the daylight and move quietly at night.

Of course, she only knew one road—from the plantation to the church. She'd been to the Miller's store and Doc Baldwin's home, but she hadn't really been anywhere else. Anthony had been all the way to Winchester, so perhaps he also knew a few hiding spots. Or maybe they could all head to the North Star and find that train.

I's sick an tired of waitin an worryin bout Anthony, bout Sam, bout George, Marcus, Milly, Mary, Lil Anthony, Maria, Westley an Elias—anytime dey outta my sight. What ifs dey gonna look some white man wrong in de face or sass somebody de wron way. I worry de same fo

Elijah an Emily when dey get oldah. I wanna be alone wid my husband. Instead, I gotta be nuhs, maid, cook, an de Lawd knows what else fo Mastah Isaac.

* * * *

Judah had been born into a culture that taught its children to honor all living beasts; even those about to be eaten. It was respectful to eat the whole animal.

But white folks had a different culture. Judah saw all the scraps coming down on the trays, the wasted food. She understood that was the reason slaves started eating chitterlings. When Master Hite gave his slaves their food rations for the month, he had Judah include the scraps of any meat his family didn't want, things they didn't find acceptable.

He give us scraps.

As much as she hated Master Hite, he was far better than Master Shields.

Least sometimes Mastah Hite try to do good.

Before planting season, Hite purchased seeds that his workers could plant for themselves. Judah was thrilled when he bought back some benne seeds. They could be eaten raw, toasted over the fire, and sometimes boiled into soups and stews. Occasionally, she would put the seeds on top of the bread when it was baking.

Judah also requested red pea seeds.

"Dey is a tiny red bean dat has a thin but stron shell, Mastah. De insides is sweet an taste like buttah when it's cooked."

She didn't tell him the real reason she wanted those

peas.

I eat dose peas when I's a chile . . . remind me a home, my beauful Africa.

That's the same way Aunt Jane had talked the first time Judah created okra stew.

"Chile, I ain't taste nothin like dis since bin home," she had said. "What you know bout cookin like dis? You's jes a youngin. Somebody taught you good."

Thank you, Aunt Sally.

Aunt Jane had asked how Judah prepared her stew.

"I mix up some vegetables and throw in some sassafrass powder for thickenin. An did you know dat okra help big women delivah dere babies?"

"Well, givin birth or not, it sho is good."

Another fan of Judah's cooking, though she didn't always want to admit it, was Miss Ann. She loved goober pea stew, which Judah's mama had cooked all the time in Goga. Judah only made it a couple times each year.

When it goober pea stew time, Missus Ann lick de bowl clean.

* * * *

It had been difficult for Judah to think about cooking or caring for anybody else since she'd heard Master Hite's plans to give away her children. She was thankful they weren't going to the market to be sold off to God knows where, but thinking about life without her children made Judah fearful and sick to her stomach. What if she would never see them again? And, it was little comfort they would now be owned by Master Hite's children.

233

Young Mastah Walker got a mean streak. He may not be as nice a mastah as his pa.

-ɜ2-

I n early August, Judah realized she was pregnant. She couldn't wait to break the news to Anthony, but he had not been home for two weeks and she was becoming worried.

It was twilight when Judah called the children inside, leaving the door open to hopefully catch a stray breeze. As always, chatter filled the cabin, Judah's eyes heavy from the long day.

Suddenly, a dark presence stood in the doorway. Young Emmanuel came into the cabin wringing his hands. His face looked pitiful, like he didn't know what to do or say.

"What wron?" Judah asked.

"I's sorry for interruptin your rest, Miss Judah, but I thought you'd want to know."

"Know what? You givin me a big fright, Emmanuel. What goin on?"

He grabbed her hands and held them in his.

"Judah, I so sorry . . . Anthony's daid."

"What?!"

Judah felt like a jagged spike had just been shoved into her chest. She could hardly breathe. The world turned strangely slow, almost hollow. Her eyes darted around the cabin, clicking on surreal scenes . . . the children scream-ing and crying, Emmanuel's frightened face, her hand shaking uncontrollably.

"Daid? How?"

"Doan really know," said Emmanuel. "It jes happen. I doan know if Mastah even knows yet. But de slave catchas say he run away an dey get im."

"Ran away? I doan understan. He wooden runaway witout tellin me."

"Dat's what I hear. One story is de catchas get him in Pennsylvania and bring him back to Woodstock. Nother says he caught leavin Westminstah and dey mistake him fo nother fella an whipped him so badly, he died on the post still strung up."

"Oh, Lawd, Anthony!" You would have thought Judah's screams would make the news untrue. "What I'm gon' do witout Anthony!"

She picked up Emily from the vegetable basket crib and squeezed her to her chest. And just as quickly as he appeared, Emmanuel was gone, undoubtedly realizing that he had just shattered Judah's entire world.

For the longest time, Judah wandered about the cabin, dazed. She couldn't think of anything except Anthony. She couldn't feel strength in her legs or arms. Sure, she cooked because that's what the cook does, but she wondered if her pies were salty because she'd cried into every single one of them. Emily tried to make Judah sit down and rest, but she couldn't. Anthony was dead.

And now in her belly was a child he would never see. Another life being born into slavery, growing up to toil for the white man.

Judah had always beamed when carrying a new life within her, but the joy of motherhood was now absent.

Judah's twelfth child, Jonathan, was born in late February 1836. Judah's energy did not return.

* * * *

"Miss Ann, I's worried bout Judah," Truelove said with concern. "She doan look good. She jes settin in dat chair an drool comin down her face. She mumblin something under her breath an she ain't takin care of her chillun much neither."

Miss Ann came down to the winter kitchen, Emily giving a worried look from the hearth.

"Judah, you feeling any better?" asked Miss Ann.

Judah barely raised her head.

"Truelove, let's get her out to her cabin. Emily, let me know if you need anything. Just make sure dinner is on time."

Since Jonathan's birth five weeks earlier, Emily had taken over most of the cooking while Judah sat in the chair and silently watched all the activity. Everyone seemed satisfied with the job she had done under such stress.

At the cabin, her daughters fed her soup and whatever Emily cooked for Judah. Marie cried as she fed her mother. As drool and food fell from Judah's mouth, Marie would whisper, "Mama, you gon be alright. You gots to be."

Sam and George entered the cabin from their long day of work, sitting on their knees in front of their mother.

Judah barely raised her head and smiled.

"Ayinde, Chaminuka . . . my boys."

"Ayinde, Chaminuka? asked Sam. "What you mean, Mama?"

They thought she whispered praise and something about a king.

THE END

ACKNOWLEDGEMENTS

The author is incredibly indebted to the current executive director of Belle Grove, Kristen O. Laise for her tireless efforts and willingness to unearth the history, however negative it may be.

Shannon Moeck of the National Park Service keeps the Judah story alive as she interprets "Kneading in Silence: A Glimpse into the Life of Judah the Enslaved Cook" numerous times throughout the year.

I salute the important work of the Slave Dwelling Project and its founder, Joseph McGill for endeavoring to protect the history of extant slave dwellings. It was through a partnership between Bloomsburg University, SDP, and Belle Grove that I first heard of Judah.

I also want to thank the members of the West Branch Christian Writers group for their constant encouragement and the Kingdom Writers group for holding me accountable to the completion of this story.

POSTSCRIPT

While based on true events with real people, this book is fiction. Much of the historical record is made of details from primary sources, but the author has taken significant license with story creation. Isaac Hite, for instance, was not a clergyman. He was given the calling of a reverend to deliver a means to discuss Christian complicity in the slave trade and its legacy. The African slave trade in America, in many ways, was supported by the Christian church. Many slavers were merely "doing their Christian duty." Martin Luther King, Jr. famously indicated how 11:00 AM on Sunday morning is the most segregated hour of the week. Sadly, in 2019, that may still be true. There exists today an important call for churches in America to openly discuss the vestiges of racism left in our society and to foster environments to candidly talk about race from the pulpits to the pews.

We do not know the identity of the father(s) of Judah's first three children—Sam, George, and Marcus. The rape of enslaved women by their white masters and captors is highly supported by research and first-hand accounts. So is the fact that families were often torn apart in the slave-buying process. Keeping Judah's family intact was useful to support the "benevolent master" narrative. The author hopes you, the reader, understand that the idea of a "good slaver" versus a "bad slaver" belief only supports white supremacy. The entire system of slavery was abhorrent writ large.

WHAT WE KNOW

Judah died April 2, 1836. Her life is mentioned in Ann Tunstall Hite's letter mourning the loss of her cook and the Hite Family Commonplace Book (1776-1859), in which the "List of Enslaved" presumed Judah ("Judy") was born in 1794 and had been purchased with two sons from Abraham Bowman.

Ann Hite's Letter to a Friend

April 5, 1836

During the last two weeks my cook was dangerously ill with a complaint one of great suffering a violent pleurisy in the first instance terminating in an inflammation of the heart which was most distressing. She finally went under the disease on Saturday morning leaving 12 children; the youngest is only 5 weeks old. I deplore her loss to her younger children more than my own inconvenience which is very considerable—but it is the will of him that cannot err of course 'it is wisest best.' I shall endeavor to discharge the additional duties that devolve upon me to the best of my ability.

Ever your attached friend,
A. T. Hite

Judah's Children

What is known about Judah's twelve children comes mainly from the Hite Family Commonplace Book and Isaac Hite Jr.'s estate upon his death in November 1836.

Sam is listed as having been born in May 1814 and that he arrived at Belle Grove after being sold by Abraham

Bowman. There are no further records about Sam, but Judah and her two sons must have been purchased in late 1816 or early 1817 since her third child (Marcus) is listed as being born on the plantation.

George (born March 1816) was given in 1836 to Walker Hite, who was 25 when his father died. The 1850 slave schedule notes that Walker owned a black man about 34 years old.

Marcus (August 1817) was valued at $1,000 in Isaac Hite's estate inventory. Marcus would be given to Cornelius Hite, who was 18 when his father died. In 1841, Cornelius would die at the age of 23, his estate listing "Marcus 24 years old $600." Accounting notes that $1,326 was received "for proceeds of sales of negros," but it does not list Marcus by name nor note to whom he was sold.

Milly (1819) was 17 when Master Hite died and given to Hugh Hite with a value of $750. She would be the last of Judah's children to not be listed with an exact birthdate.

Mary (March 6, 1821) was valued at $750 when she was 15 and noted to be "diseased."

Anthony (February 1823) was given to Walker Hite sometime after 1836. The 1850 slave schedule notes that Walker owned a black man about Anthony's age.

Maria (February 15, 1825) who had been valued at $600 when she was 11, would give birth to four children, all born after their grandmother's death—Emelia (Sept. 4, 1844), Amanda (Jan. 28, 1847), Willis (Aug. 31, 1848) and Ann Eliza (Jan. 25, 1850). Amanda died as a young child.

It is frustrating that we don't more about Maria's life or her children. We do know that her fourth child was born before Ann Hite's death in 1851, but Maria and her family are not listed among the four enslaved people in Ann's estate inventory. There are no notes about Maria and her children being sold or given to any family members. If Isaac is dead, who is recording these names in the Hite records? Ann? Her son Isaac Fontaine Hite who may have been doing some farming and milling at Belle Grove? He did make a list of "my negros" in 1851, but neither Maria nor her children are mentioned.

Westley (September 1, 1827) also became lost to history. Valued at $600 in Isaac's estate, he was "given to Hugh." However, there is no man of Westley's age listed in the 1850 slave schedule for Hugh Holmes Hite.

Elias (March 16, 1830) is only listed in the Isaac Hite's inventory, a notation that the six-year-old Elias carried a $450 value.

Elijah (January 4, 1832) was only four years old when his mother died. The Commonplace Book notes that the Elijah was "Given to Cornelius, sold bought by A.T. Hite." The phrase of "sold bought" is confusing. We do know that Ann Hite's estate in 1851 lists only four enslaved people, but no ages—Elijah $800, Jim (Blacksmith) $450, Sally (a cook) $175, and Martha (Sally's child) $250. We gather that Cornelius' estate sold Elijah back to Ann, but it is curious that the document states "received by cash of Ann T. Hite for Negro Jim." Why was Jim mentioned by name and the other enslaved people once owned by Cornelius were not? Still, there is the notation "sold bought by A. T. Hite" and he was listed in her estate inventory.

Emily (May 13, 1834) would be listed in Isaac Hite's estate inventory with a $150 value. There are no further records.

Jonathan (February 28, 1836) was Judah's youngest child and would not have lived a year. We do not know if he died before his mother in April, but he was not alive by Isaac's death in November.

The Enslaved

The people from Belle Grove were real–Truelove, Anthony, Suze, Nancy . . . unfortunately, it is impossible now to know Judah's circle of friends other than her children. Anthony, born in 1789, was selected to play the role of her husband and father to her kids. Truelove, born in 1783, might have made a great housemaid.

This I do know: enslaved folks created authentic lives amid the chaos and uncertainly of the slave system. This story seeks to affirm and honor that humanity.

The White Folks

While James Shields was fictional, we do know that Abraham Bowman would sell Judah, Sam, and George to Isaac Hite.

Isaac Hite Jr. (1758-1836) fought for the Continental Army during the Revolutionary War. He was given the rank of major for his service to the Virginia Militia after the war. A graduate of William and Mary College, he married Nelly Madison in 1783 and was deeded 483 acres (the original Belle Grove) by his father and given 15 slaves by her father. As his grain and livestock business grew, Hite would eventually obtain 7,500 acres. He also owned a general store, gristmill, sawmill, and distillery. During his lifetime, he owned 276 African-American men, women, and children. At his death in November 1836,

Isaac's estate inventory listed 44 enslaved people for a total value of $16,150 ($418,708 today). The estate also listed livestock, farming utensils, house and kitchen furniture at about the same amount.

Ann Tunstall Maury Hite (1782-1851) was the daughter of a reverend who married Isaac after the death of his first wife in 1802. Together, they had 10 children—Ann (1805-33), Isaac (1807-1884), Mary (1808-56), Rebecca (1810-51), Walker (1811-90), Sarah (1812-96), Penelope (1814-38), Hugh (1816-87), Cornelius (1818-41), and Matilda (1819-53). Ann and Judah would have been pregnant together several times. Nine years after Ann's death, Belle Grove was sold out of the Hite family.

Nelly Madison Hite (1760-1802) was the younger sister of future president James Madison. One of her three children—James (1798-91)—passed away prior to her death. Her daughter, Nelly, who was born in 1789, would live until 1830. Her son, also named James, lived from 1793-1860.

Abraham Bowman (1749-1837) was a colonel in the Continental Army, a frontiersman, and prominent Kentucky landowner. Born near Strasburg, Virginia, he was Isaac Hite's cousin. Among the earliest settlers in Kentucky, Abraham was a close friend of Daniel Boone.

James Madison (1751-1836) was a Founding Father and fourth president of the United States from 1809 to 1817. A gifted writer, statesman, and philosopher, Madison is considered the "Father of the Constitution" for his work on the U.S. Constitution, Bill of Rights, and The Federalist Papers. Born into a wealthy Virginia family, he was the older brother of Eleanor "Nelly" Hite.

Elijah Lovejoy (1802-1837) was a Presbyterian minister, journalist and abolitionist from Maine. On November 9, 1837, two days shy of his thirty-fifth birthday, he was attacked, shot and killed by a pro-slavery mob in Alton, Illinois.

The Commonplace Book

From the time of his Revolutionary War service, Major Isaac Hite recorded important details of his life in his Commonplace Book. His financial and genealogical records, as well as his thoughts on political issues, reveals much about his character. Many of the sections Hite hand-copied his thoughts on war, marriage, parental power, and slavery.

In the book, Hite documented the types of civil power that masters held over their domestics. In his estimation, the servant was deemed to have consented to his or her slavery as far as it was managed consistently with humanity. To Hite, the children of all slaves were born free, but subject to many disadvantages from the miserable situation of their parents—the mother's loss of work and risk of life giving birth to that child, the cost to the master of maintaining the child, and the hazard of their dying as to how the loss would affect their master. Hite believed it was the duty of servants to perform their work with diligence and fidelity as it was the duty of masters to abstain from all cruelty and insolence, remembering that everyone must give an account of his conduct to God, the common parent of all.

Emanuel Jackson's Family

Emanuel Jackson did, in fact, finance the manumission of his son, Emmanuel Jr., from the heirs of the late Isaac Hite of Virginia for the sum of $800. In Allegheny County (PA), Jackson Sr. freed his son.

It did not stop there. It appears that the free-black father arranged through Isaac Fontaine Hite for the sale of another son, Daniel Jackson, along with his wife and children. They would all live in Pittsburgh. The records at Belle Grove indicate that Emanuel would also purchase his daughter Betsy Ann and son Frank. Hannah, who was enslaved at Belle Grove, is listed as the mother of these children.

Belle Grove

Belle Grove is recognized as a National Park Service historical site and actively maintains its historical presence through tours of the grounds and manor house.

The plantation also serves as an educational facility. Students from elementary through high school in the surrounding region experience field trips to hear the docents tell the Belle Grove story.

During the Civil War, the plantation figured as pivotal site with the Battle at Cedar Creek. According to the Belle Grove website, "after a surprise attack by Confederate General Jubal Early in the early hours of October 19, 1864, General Sheridan quickly regained the territory, securing the valley for the Union and boosting President Abraham Lincoln's chances for re-election."

Visit the Belle Grove Plantation website at www.belle-grove.org.

RECIPES

Food, in some ways, has a direct line to our memories. I especially love cookbooks that share stories, not just detailed recipes.

During a visit by my mother several years ago, she began rifling through my cookbook collection. While thumbing through Ernest Mickler's *White Trash Cooking*, she suddenly began to cry. When I inquired about the tears, she showed me an enclosed recipe for Slumgullion, a leftovers casserole where you put in whatever you have. When I was growing up, my mother called it "Shush, Let's Make a Meal." It was a dish she had learned from her mother. My grandmother died when I was four years old, but in that moment, I had never felt so close to her.

These are recipes for dishes Judah likely would have prepared for her enslavers. None of the recipes provide specific amounts of ingredients. Cooking, for the uneducated enslaved woman, would likely have been a repeated task of trial and error while she learned to perfect her dishes to her master's tastes and desires.

RHUBARB JELLY
Wash and cut rhubarb into inch lengths. Place in preserving kettle. Add enough water to prevent from sticking. Cook slowly in covered kettle until soft. Strain through jelly bag. Measure 1 c. juice and add 2 tbs. cornstarch and stir vigorously. Bring to boil. Add 1 c. honey and continue to boil until jelly test is secured. Fill hot glasses or jars with the jelly and cover with melted paraffin.

SASSAFRASS JELLY

Boil sassafrass roots for one half hour and strain. Measure 2 cups of this tea into pan. Add some pectin and just bring barely to a boil. Add 3 cups of honey (without the comb) and grated sassafrass root bark. Simmer six minutes. Fill hot glasses or jars with the jelly and cover with melted paraffin.

PORK PIE

Pare and thinly slice 6 potatoes, chop 1 onion. Butter a baking dish, place one layer of potatoes on the bottom and sprinkle with onions. Spread with a layer of cold roast pork and repeat. Cover with milk. Bake in hot oven for an hour.

CHICKEN AND DUMPLINGS

Stew chicken. When tender, pick the meat from the bones. Put meat in a large pan with tight fitting lid and add four cups of broth, the boiling liquid. Bring to a boil. For the dumplings: 1 1/2 cups flour, 3 tbs. baking powder, 3/4 tsp. salt, 1 1/2 tbs. lard, 3/4 c. milk.

Sift together the dry ingredients and cut in the lard. Stir in enough milk, mixing only to moisten the dough thoroughly. Drop by teaspoons into boiling chicken broth. Dip the spoon into the boiling liquid first so that the dough will slide off easily. Cover pan tightly and cook fifteen minutes.

HOG JOWLS AND TURNIP GREENS

Mustard, kale, and turnip greens are cooked same as spinach. Smoked hog jowl is cooked with greens. Season well with red pepper and salt. Cook until tender, drain and serve on platter with meat in center and poached eggs. Always serve with cornbread.

BAKED BEETS

Dice 6 or 8 beets in a casserole. Mix two tbs. flour, one half c. sugar, one half tsp. salt, one quarter c. water, one half c. vinegar, one tbs. butter. Pour over beets. Bake in bean pot at 350° for one hour.

DANDELION GREENS

They can be used until they bloom. Pick over carefully, wash in several waters. Put in boiling water with a piece of salt pork. Boil one hour. Drain well. Add salted boiling water, boil two more hours. When well done and tender, turn into colander and drain.

OAT PANCAKES

Ingredients: 1 c. flour, 1/2 tsp. salt, 1 c. milk, 2 tsp. baking powder, 1/2 c. oats, 1 egg, 2 tbs. butter. Beat egg with milk. Combine with dry ingredients. Melt butter and stir into batter. Pour 1/3 c. batter on hot griddle for each cake. Add butter to griddle as needed. Cook until bubbles form and hold and the cake is light brown. Turn. Brown other side. Serve warm with maple syrup and butter.

MINCEMEAT

Ingredients: 4 cups dried apples (cooked), 1 hog head, 1 to 2 quarts juice or brandy, 5 lbs. sugar, 12 oranges (peeled, seeded, chopped), 1 lb. raisins. Soak hog head overnight. Remove eyes, ears, and snout. With an ax, split the top away from the jowls (note: don't skin the jowls but remove meat from bones, salt it down and save it for a special New Year's dinner). Cook a slab of it with black-eyed peas and serve with boiled cabbage, cornbread and milk. Use the top part of the head for mincemeat.

Cook in a large kettle, covered, on medium heat until it starts to boil, then on medium-low for a good simmer for 2 or 3 hours until tender. Remove meat from bones and chop real coarse-like. Add raisins, cooked dried apples, oranges, sugar, and grape juice. Put it all in the pot. Stir almost constantly, like we do with the apple butter. Simmer and stir until thick enough to be used as pie filling.

CORN BREAD

Ingredients: 1 c. corn meal, 2 eggs, 1/2 c. flour, 1/3 c. shortening, 2 tsp. sugar, 1/4 tsp. soda. Add enough buttermilk to make soft dough, then beat and mix together. Bake in greased iron skillet.

COUNTRY PICKLES

Small, raw whole cucumbers with salt, vinegar, sugar. Clean the cucumbers and fill as many jars as needed. Add to each jar 1/2 c. sugar, one teaspoon salt, and enough vinegar to bring liquid up to the halfway mark. Finish filling each jar with water. Seal the lids.

PIE CRUST

3/4 c. lard, 1 tbs. milk, 1/4 c. boiling water, 2 c. flour, 1 tsp. salt. Put lard in medium sized bowl. Add water and milk. Break up lumps with a fork. Tilt bowl and beat with fork in cross the bowl strokes until mixture is smooth like whipped cream and holds soft peaks. Sift flour and salt on top of mixture. With vigorous, round the bowl strokes, stir quickly, forming dough that clings together and cleans bowl. Pick up dough and work into a smooth, round ball. Divide in half. Roll out on floured board. Lift and sprinkle flour under it if it tends to stick. Roll out crust to 1/8-inch thickness. Do not grease pie pan but dust flour over it lightly. Trim excess dough from outside edges with a knife. Prick holes around sides and in the center with fork. Bake for 12 to 15 minutes to a light brown.

PICKLED OKRA

1 qt. fresh whole okra pods, 2 tbs. salt, 1 tsp. pickling spices, 1 c. sugar, 1 c. vinegar. Wash and pick over young whole okra pods. Soak overnight in salt water. Drain. Add vinegar, sugar, and spices and enough water to cover. Bring to a boil. Cook on a slow boil for five minutes. Pack in jars and seal.

SORGHUM CAKE

1/2 c. sorghum, 1 c. sugar, 2 tsp. soda, 2 1/4 c. flour, 1/2 c. butter, 1/2 tsp. cinnamon. Cream the butter and sugar together. Add sorghum and mix. Sift together the flour, soda, and cinnamon and stir into the creamed mixture. Just before pouring into a greased baking pan, stir one cup of boiling water into batter. It will foam up. Bake until done (when it springs back after being pressed lightly with fingertips).

RICE CUSTARD

2 eggs lightly beaten, 1 1/2 c. milk, 1/8 tsp. salt, 2 c. cooked rice, 1 tsp. vanilla, 1/3 c. raisins, 1/8 tsp. cinnamon, 2 tbs. honey or sugar. Mix together. Put in baking dish or pan, covered. Bake 45 minutes at 350°.

GLAZED APPLES

Using one apple per serving, wash, core, and slice 1/4 inch thick. Heat skillet with cookin' grease in de bottom. Spread apple slices out in one layer. When one side is brown, turn. Place 1/2 teaspoon of sugar on each browned side. When the other side is brown, the sugar will be melted. Finish with a sprinkling of cinnamon.

BEAN SOUP

1 lb. dried navy beans, 1 tsp. flour, 2 tbs. butter, 1/2 onion minced, 1/2 tsp. salt, dash of pepper, 1 hambone. Soak beans in water for at least 4 hours, but overnight is better. Drain off. Cover with boiling water. Add hambone and cook gently for 35 minutes. Drain off again. Add fresh water. Cut meat from bone and add it to the soup. Give bone to the dog. In a small pan blend together and cook flour with butter, then stir it into the beans along with salt, pepper, and onion. Simmer about 40 minutes until beans are soft.

PICKLED CORN ON THE COB

Corn on the cob, 20-gallon jar or crock, pickling salt, clean feed sack, clean rock. Pick corn fresh from patch, shuck it an' boil it for five minutes. Remove from heat and plunge into cold water. Lay it out on a clean towel. Then put the corn inside a clean feed sack. Dissolve one handful pickling salt for each gallon of cold water needed to cover contents. Lay a clean rock on top of the corn. Every 3 or 4 days skim the scum off the top. Corn should be ready to eat in 2 or 3 weeks.

CORN PONE

1 c. corn meal, 1 tsp. salt, 3/4 c. boiling water, 1 tbs. lard. Combine the meal and salt. While blending, gradually add the water. Melt the lard in the baking pan. After pan is greased, pour extra into the mix and blend. The mix should not be more than one inch thick in the baking pan to start with. It will rise very little. (To make it rise like cornbread, add two teaspoons of baking powder.) The pone will develop a rich, brown, crunchy crust. It should bake about 50 to 60 minutes. Could be fried on a griddle or hung on the hearth. Serve with greens and salt pork.

APPLE PAN DOWDY

6 medium size tart apples, 1/4 tsp. nutmeg, 1/2 c. molasses, 1/4 tsp. salt, 1 tsp. cinnamon, 1/2 c. butter, 2 tsp. baking powder, 1 c. flour, 3/4 c. milk, 1 1/2 tbs. butter. Peel and core apples and cut them into eighths. Oil a deep baking dish and place apple pieces in it. Cover with molasses, cinnamon, sugar, and nutmeg. Then melt the half cup of butter. Mix with milk. Stir baking powder and

salt into flour and cut in the 1 ½ tablespoons of butter. Spread over the apples. Bake at 325° for 30 minutes. Break the topping with a fork, working it among the apples. Put back in thre oven and bake another half hour. Serve with cream.

HOPPIN' JOHN

2 c. cooked black-eyed peas, 2 hot peppers (chopped), 1 1/2 c. whole grain rice, 1 tbs. butter. Cook rice and peppers. Mix with black-eyed peas and butter.

SALT RISING BREAD

2 cups milk, 1/2 tsp. salt, 2 cups corn meal, 1/2 tsp. baking soda, 2 tsp. sugar, 8-10 cups flour, 2 tbs. shortening. Heat milk to scalding point. Remove from heat. Add in the cornmeal while stirring the milk, sugar, and salt. Stir until smooth. Cover with a tea towel and set in a warm place overnight. Next morning, add one cup of warm water mixed with baking soda and about 2 1/2 cups of flour (enough to make a rather stiff dough). Set the bowl in a pan of warm water, cover and let stand until it foams up. This can take from two hours to half a day. Try to keep the water at an even temperature all the time—not too hot, not too cold. If it seems as though the batter is not rising, give it a stir to help it along. Some people object to the odor during this period but it is the sour fermentation which causes it. But the more you have of it, the more sure you are of having sweet bread when it is baked.

When the batter has risen, knead in the shortening and more flour (it may take as much as 8 cups) to make a stiff dough. Shape into two loaves, set in greased loaf pans and let it rise until double in size. Bake in a preheated 350° oven for approximately one hour or until light brown.

POTATO BISCUITS

1 c. mashed potatoes, 1 tbs. honey, 2 tbs. butter, 2 c. flour, 1/2 tsp. soda, 2 tbs. baking powder, 1 c. buttermilk, 1 tbs. brown sugar. Stir butter into potatoes. Dissolve soda in buttermilk, add honey. Mix baking powder, sugar, flour, adding in milk as you go. Press into 3/4-inch pad, cut biscuits. Bake at 400°.

WILTED LETTUCE AND ONION SALAD

Dressing: 2 tbs. melted bacon grease, 2 tbs. vinegar, 1 tbs. sugar. Heat to boiling point and pour over 1 1/2 quarts shredded lettuce, 3 chopped green onions. Add salt and pepper to taste. Toss to mix. Serve at once.

BREAD AND BUTTER PICKLES

Use 4 quarts, medium sized cucumbers. Slice thin but do not peel. Add 6 medium white onions (sliced thin); 2 chopped green peppers, and 3 whole garlic cloves. Add 1/3 c. salt and mix thoroughly. Let stand covered for four hours. Drain well. Combine 5 c. sugar, 1 1/2 tsp. turmeric, 1 1/2 tsp. celery seed, 2 tbs. mustard seed, 3 c. vinegar. Pour over cucumbers. Heat to boiling point. Seal in hot jars.

MOLASSES CANDY

2 c. molasses, 1 c. sugar, 1 tbs. vinegar. Cook together until crunchy or brittle when dropped in cold water. Stir in a pinch of baking soda and three cups of chopped black walnuts. Pour in greased pan. Break into pieces when cold.

PICKLED PEACHES

One pint cooked peach halves. To the syrup, add 3/4 c. firmly packed brown sugar, 1/2 c. vinegar, two 3-inch cinnamon sticks, 1 tsp. whole cloves, 1 tsp. allspice. Boil five minutes. Add the peach halves and simmer another five minutes. Chill overnight. Delicious with meats or on a party plate.

WATERMELON RIND PICKLES

2 qts. diced watermelon rind, 1 c. vinegar, 1 tbs. lime juice, 2 c. sugar. Add rind and lime juice to a quart of water and soak overnight. Rinse rind, drain and cook in water for an hour or until tender. Then mix sugar and vinegar and add to the rind. Simmer mixture for ten minutes and set aside for one night. Fill jars with mixture. Boil one-quart vinegar until clear and thick. Add to rind in jars and seal.

SPOON BREAD

Stir together: 1 c. yellow corn meal, 1 1/2 tsp. baking powder, 1/2 tsp. salt. In greased casserole dish, pour: 2 eggs (beaten), 3 tbs. melted butter. In medium sized pan, heat: 2 1/4 c. milk (stir to avoid scorching). As it starts boiling, sprinkle in the dry ingredients, stirring vigorously with wooden spoon. Cook and stir for two or three minutes, as it thickens. Mix with eggs in the casserole. Bake at 425° for 45 minutes. Serve from casserole with a spoon. Eat with a fork.

PEPPER HASH

Wash, remove seeds, and chop 1 dozen sweet red peppers, 1 dozen sweet green peppers, 1 dozen small green onions. Add 3 tsp. Salt and cook slowly for ten minutes. Drain and add 4 c. mild vinegar and 1 c. brown sugar. Bring to boiling point and seal in jars.

APPLE RELISH

Grind 2 hot peppers and 5 onions. Add 1 tsp. salt. Add one cup boiling water. Let it stand 15 minutes and drain. Add 14 large red apples that have been chopped with the skins left on (core removed, of course). 1-quart vinegar, 1 c. sugar, cloth bag with allspice, a spoon of cloves, and a cinnamon stick. Cook 10-15 minutes. Seal in jars.

APPLE PIE

3 or 4 large tart apples, 1/2 c. sugar, 2 tbs. flour, 1/2 tsp. nutmeg, 2 tbs. lemon juice, 1/2 c. sugar, 1/2 c. flour, 1 stick butter. Pare and slice apples in large bowl. Mix sugar, flour, and nutmeg and sprinkle over apple slices. Drizzle with lemon juice. Toss to cover completely with the juice. Place in pie shell. Combine 1/2 c. sugar and 1/2 c. flour in small bowl. Cut up the butter and sprinkle over apples. Bake for an hour.

GREEN TOMATO PIE

Wash and thinly slice 3 cups green tomatoes. Mix together with 1 1/2 c. sugar, 1/4 tsp. cinnamon, 1/4 tsp. salt, 5 tbs. lemon juice, 5 tsp. grated lemon rind, 2 tbs. butter. Arrange tomatoes in layers, sprinkling each layer with a mixture of the other ingredients in unbaked pe shell. Add top crust and bake for 35 to 40 minutes.

VINEGAR PIE

1 egg, 4 tbs. flour, 3 tbs. vinegar, 1 c. sugar, 1 tsp. lemon, 1 c. boiling water, 1 baked pie shell. Mix together sugar and flour. Add boiling water. Cook five minutes. Add beaten egg. Cook two minutes. Add lemon and vinegar. Put in pie shell, cool.

SWEET POTATO PIE

3 medium sweet potatoes, 1/4 tsp. nutmeg, 1 tsp. baking powder, 1/2 c. milk, 1/4 c. butter, 1 tsp. brandy, 2 eggs (separated), 1/2 c. honey, 1/4 tsp. salt. Scrub potatoes and place in pan. Cover with boiling water, heat to boil. Cook until potatoes are soft. Drain potatoes, skin while hot. Cool slightly. Beat in butter and remaining ingredients. Pour mixture in pot and bake on high heat for 15 minutes and lower temp for 30 minutes. You can beat the whites with sugar to make a meringue. Spread over pie making sure meringue touches crust all around and is smooth or swirled over top. Return to heat to brown meringue. Remove and cool.

ABOUT THE AUTHOR

Brian C. Johnson honors the struggles and accomplishments of the ordinary citizens who launched the Civil Rights Movement by committing himself personally and professionally to the advancement of multicultural and inclusive education.

He has served as a faculty member in the department of academic enrichment at Bloomsburg University of Pennsylvania and was the director of the Frederick Douglass Institute for Academic Excellence. He is a founder of the Pennsylvania Association of Liaisons and Officers of Multicultural Affairs, a consortium that promotes best practices in higher education. He earned both bachelor's and master's degrees in English from California University of Pennsylvania and a PhD at Indiana University of Pennsylvania in Communications Media and Instructional Technology. His research examines the role of mainstream film in the development of social dominance orientation.

Johnson serves on the ministry team at Revival Tabernacle in Watsontown, PA where he is a church elder, youth minister, and leads the Kingdom Writers' guild. He is a film reviewer for Christian Spotlight on Entertainment. He and his wife, Darlene, have four children—Kasey, Thomas, Aubyn, and Analisa.

Printed in Great Britain
by Amazon